Eat, Drink, and Be Scary

Eat, Drink, and Be Scary

A Ravenmist Whodunit
Book One

By Olivia Jaymes

www.OliviaJaymes.com

EAT, DRINK, AND BE SCARY
Copyright © 2019 by Olivia Jaymes
Print Edition

Eat, Drink, and Be Scary

Welcome to Ravenmist! A tiny Midwestern town with charming covered bridges, quirky residents, delightful antique shops, and more than their share of haunted activity.

It's time for the annual Fall Festival, and that means the quaint Ravenmist Inn – owned by Theodosia "Tedi" Hamilton – is filled to the brim with out of town guests. It's her favorite time of the year with all the spooky decorations, sugar-filled candy, and over the top costumes.

The festival doesn't quite go as planned, however, when one of her guests is found face down in the apple bob. To make things worse, her best friend becomes the number one suspect. Tedi has no choice but to spring into action.

Come join the spirited antics as Tedi deals with an unsolved murder, a shy ghost in her closet, a mischievous spirit in the bookstore, and the handsome new local sheriff who drives her crazy. You see, he thinks all the ghost stories are made up for the tourists. But Tedi knows better, and now so will you…

Chapter One

THE NEXT TWENTY-FOUR hours were going to suck. There was no avoiding this fact. I'd been through this four times before, so at least I knew what to expect. Mayhem. Complete and total, not just a little bit. The whole town of Ravenmist was in chaos because it was the weekend of the annual fall festival, scheduled just a week before Halloween.

In Ravenmist, Halloween just might be the most important day of the year. It was certainly the most fun.

Before we get too far, I should probably introduce myself. My name is Tedi Hamilton and I own the Ravenmist Inn, which has been in my father's family for generations. It's a large, rambling Victorian with several buildings on the property that had been painstakingly cared for over the years. My grandmother Rose used to run it and now I do.

Nice to meet you. Glad you stopped by.

Tedi is short for Theodosia by the way, but only my mother calls me that. When she's really ticked off at me she'll call me by my whole name, which is Theodosia Elizabeth Virginia Evans Hamilton. I'm pretty sure my Southern born and bred mother would have named me Scarlett if she thought she could get away with it, but she did saddle me with Theodosia. Luckily my father, a no-nonsense Midwesterner, immediately dubbed me Tedi and a nickname was born.

I needed an industrial strength cup of coffee and a cruller more than I needed to breathe. Unfortunately, I wasn't going to get either until I dealt with the angry man on the other side of the front desk of my inn. Customer service is so rewarding.

"I have a reservation," the middle-aged man snarled, his face getting red. He slapped his hand on the counter, the sunlight catching on his expensive gold and diamond watch and sending a blinding flash into my eyes. While some people might have gone for class and taste, this timepiece seemed more like a monument to wealth. In other words, it was ugly. A big chunk of precious metal on display. "I want to go up to my room now. I have work to do."

"I understand that, sir," I replied in my most soothing tone. Missy was going to be so proud of how I'd kept my temper. She was always encouraging me to chill out and relax. I did like to kick back but it was usually with an old movie and a glass of wine. "But check-in time is three in the afternoon. It is currently nine-thirty in the morning. The people in your room are still asleep or eating breakfast. They have until eleven to check out. I can take your bags and store them until check-in time while you spend the day seeing the beautiful sights of Ravenmist."

My soon to be guest was not amused, nor was he soothed by my tone of voice. I might have to bring out the big guns if he didn't quiet down. The Ravenmist Inn prided itself on being a haven from the hustle and bustle of the regular world. We were also proud of our haunted history, but that's a story for later.

The couple standing behind him stepped forward, the man nudging Mr. Entitlement's shoulder. "Just let it go, Jerry. It'll be fine. We'll walk around town and get something to eat."

The irate guest shot a quelling look over his shoulder. "I'll handle this, Roger. These people simply don't know how to run a business."

I hated to break it to this guy, but the Ravenmist Inn had been in business for over a hundred and fifty years and would probably be here a hundred and fifty years after both he and I were gone.

"My name is Jerome Bergstrom and my secretary made these reservations. She didn't tell me about any check-in time. And I don't want to walk around this backwater dot on the map. I want to work, so get me a room right now."

This was the third time good ol' Jerome had told me his name so it was deeply imprinted on my brain at this point. He didn't need to repeat it again and frankly, I didn't want him to. As for his poor secretary, whatever he was paying her it clearly wasn't enough.

Jerome was destined to be furious and unhappy because there was nothing I could do for him. He'd shown up hours early and his room simply wasn't available. I was funny and sarcastic but I wasn't a witch. I couldn't conjure a room out of thin air. If he didn't like it he was welcome to go elsewhere. On the busiest weekend of the year, I could rent his room ten times over without breaking a sweat.

"There are no rooms to put you in, Mr. Bergstrom." Inwardly I counted to ten to try and quell my own growing impatience. "You have two choices. You can wait until three or you can take your business elsewhere. Let me know what you want to do."

I said it as sweetly as possible but I stood my ground. I wasn't going to be a pushover for some guy with too much money and too little sense from the big city. I'd lived in Chicago long enough to know how these guys operated.

I waited for Jerome's head to explode in my tiny lobby, making a big mess that one of my staff would have to clean up, but the woman he was with pushed him aside and muttered something under her breath that I couldn't make out but sounded suspiciously like the words *let me handle this*.

The attractive middle-aged woman gave me a wide smile. "I'm Lorna Bergstrom and these are our friends Roger and Cherie Mullaney. We're all here for the festival. Please let me apologize for my husband. He's been under a great deal of stress these days. Of course, we're happy to wait until you have a room ready. Do you think it might be before three o'clock?"

It was possible. Anything was possible.

"I can't promise but I can try. It definitely won't be until after lunch."

The blond smiling man who had spoken before – whom I now knew was Roger Mullaney – stepped forward to the counter. His pretty wife hovered in the background, her expression anxious. "That's fine. We're early and of course it takes time to get our rooms ready. Please let me leave my phone number with you."

Mr. Mullaney slipped his business card across the desk and I quickly pocketed it.

A tall body hovered just behind the Bergstroms and I felt myself tense slightly. I knew who it was and he wasn't here to compliment the decor or to partake in the famous Ravenmist Inn waffles.

He'd only stopped by for one reason. Because he had a problem with something. He'd have to wait his turn. Jerome was trying to protest but his wife kept telling him to hush up.

Gosh, I miss being married sometimes.

That was sarcasm, by the way.

Tired of dealing with the couple, I slapped Jerome's credit card into the hand of my assistant Janie. "Please run this and get them checked in. Alan, can you take their bags and lock them in the storeroom, please?"

Both Janie and Alan leaped into action and I finally turned my attention to the glowering man in my peripheral vision.

Jackson Garrett. The new sheriff of Ravenmist, formerly of the Chicago PD. He was quickly becoming a thorn in my side about this festival. From the dark expression on his face today wasn't going to be any better than yesterday. Or the day before that.

"I'm very busy, Sheriff, so can you make this quick?"

"No."

Where in the heck was my coffee? No way was I dealing with him without a huge dose of caffeine.

"IT'S A FIRE hazard," the sheriff argued as he surveyed the back area of the inn. I had to admit that my staff had outdone themselves this year with the decorations. Spooky didn't even begin to describe what they – and myself – had achieved. "You can't have a bonfire. Someone could get hurt."

I didn't really have time for this. There were a million things on my to do list and not one of them was *get hassled by the sheriff.*

"The town of Ravenmist has had a bonfire on Fall Festival night for at least eighty years, if not more. Now you can be part of that long and proud tradition, Sheriff."

"It's dangerous."

"It's tradition. No one has been hurt in all that time."

"Then you're far overdue for something bad to happen."

Somebody's glass was only half full. He needed to lighten up.

"You're not exactly an optimist, are you? I think we're going to keep the bonfire. Alvin Hailey is in charge of it every year. He knows what he's doing."

"Alvin Hailey lives in his parents' basement and thinks the government is listening in to his conversations."

"For all we know they're listening to all of us, so choose your words carefully. Seriously, he might have a persecution complex but he does know what he's doing with the bonfire."

The sheriff scraped his hand down his red face. The towns-folk were always going on and on about how good-looking he was with his broad shoulders and dark hair. I liked blonds better, and those shoulders blocked out the sunshine.

"You don't have a permit."

"Unless the laws have changed in the last half hour, I don't need a permit. Can we move on? What else do you hate?"

He hated everything. I'd never seen a man dislike fun as much as he did.

He pointed to the patio area where there were about two dozen tables set up by a long buffet. Black tablecloths, spider webs stretched across and between the chairs. Each table was adorned with fake spiders, plastic bloody hands, and a grinning jack-o-lantern in the center that would light up after dark. The buffet was draped in orange and purple lights and flashing skulls were placed strategically along its surface. The whole section was covered with a leafy trellis but I'd gone whole hog here too, adding lights, witches, and pumpkins. The theme of the festival was autumn but the party tonight was pure Halloween. Did I mention that it was a costume party? Consider yourself cordially invited.

"You hate food and drink?"

He heaved out a great put-upon sigh. "No, I hate the bob-bing for apples game. That's a drowning hazard just waiting to happen. Some kid is going to have to be revived with CPR. I guarantee it."

Ah, the bobbing for apples game was located at the far corner of the patio and was mostly for show. Not too many people wanted to mess up their hair, makeup, or costumes just to win a small keychain.

My best friend Missy was in charge of setting the game up this afternoon and she'd done a terrific job. It was roped off with black and orange plastic streamers decorated with fake autumn leaves. She'd asked me for a glue gun earlier so I think that's how she'd attached them, although I might have recommended a stapler. She'd also draped some green twinkle lights around the area so that no one was going to miss the giant metal tub of apples up on a pedestal.

"We don't have many takers on the game. It's mostly for show, like the feats of strength sledgehammer game in the garden. How about if we put up a sign that it's for adults only? Will that make you happy?"

Garrett appeared shocked that I'd given in. His brows rose almost to his hairline and he didn't answer right away.

"I guess that would be okay. Someone will be watching it the whole time?"

"Missy says that her volunteer sign-up sheet is full so the answer is yes."

His gaze was running over the set-up, taking in all the decorations. "Do you have any trouble getting volunteers to work the festival?"

"No, they always want the t-shirt that Missy designs. You can't buy them. You can only get them if you volunteer."

"A t-shirt is that valuable?"

"Wait until you see the t-shirts. Missy is a design genius. Are we done now?"

Hope always springs eternal but I knew the answer was no. He shook his head just as someone cleared their throat behind me. I turned and Lorna Bergstrom was standing there, a nervous smile on her face.

"Hi, how can I help you?"

The woman cleared her throat again, her hands wrung together. "I just wanted to apologize for my husband's behavior earlier. He gets like that sometimes."

"Thank you but it's fine," I replied. This woman shouldn't have to apologize for her husband's actions. His jerk behavior shouldn't reflect on her. She was probably a perfectly nice person. "Did your luggage get taken care of?"

"It did, thank you. I just really wanted to say I was sorry." She looked away, her lips tightening. "My mother told me not to marry him. I should have listened to her. He's a…difficult man. Even his own children don't want to be around him."

How charming.

"It's fine," I assured her. I'd been harassed by much worse guests, including one man who had threatened me with a meat cleaver. Luckily, the former sheriff had been having lunch in my dining room and tackled the guest to the floor. "I hope you both can relax and enjoy yourselves while you're here. The festival is truly wonderful."

Lorna smiled, glancing over her shoulder to where her friends hovered several feet away. Roger Mullaney was scrolling through his phone while his wife Cherie looked decidedly bored. City people who had fooled themselves into thinking they'd enjoy a weekend in a small town.

"I'm looking forward to it. I better go, though. Jerry is off the phone now. We're going to try and take him to look into some of the antique shops. He'll hate it, though. He hates everything."

Marital bliss. I would never partake of that ever again. Once was enough.

The woman hurried away, leaving me with Garrett who still had a laundry list of complaints that we needed to go through. I checked my watch and tapped the crystal with my fingernail.

"You have ten more minutes to complain and then I need to get back to work."

"Fine. You can't have people swinging a sledgehammer all over the place. Someone is going to get hurt." He pulled a piece of paper from his shirt pocket. "I have a few more items on this list as well. I need to talk to the town council about all of this at the next meeting. I think we need to put some rules and regulations in place."

"Maybe the spirits of Ravenmist's past keep us safe."

I'd often wondered why none of the things Garrett had suggested had ever happened.

"Or maybe you've just been lucky. Now let's talk about that sledgehammer."

I guess our new sheriff didn't believe in ghosts. He'd come to the wrong town. Ravenmist was absolutely one hundred percent haunted.

Chapter Two

I'VE MENTIONED MY friend Missy Harper but I haven't really said much about her, so let me rectify that now. She and I have been best friends since grade school. We sat next to each other in kindergarten because my last name was Hamilton and hers was Harper. For the rest of our school career we were constantly next to one another, whether it was locker assignments or our graduation ceremony. So it was a good thing we liked each other so much.

She has been my friend and confidant all through school and even when we both moved away and went to different universities. Missy had come back to town after college to run the family bookstore, but I'd stayed in the city building a career at a soulless financial firm. I can't tell you the name of it but I refer to it as Beelzebub Financial. You get the idea.

I've told you how long we'd been friends, so you'll know that there isn't anything I wouldn't do for her and vice versa. Which is how I came to be wearing this sexy Little Red Riding Hood costume that she designed for me.

I stood in front of the mirror checking out my reflection. "I look ridiculous. I'm too old to carry this off."

Missy snorted and tossed her long dark hair. She had hair to die for. Long, thick, and shiny. I'd coveted it my entire life but had to settle for auburn locks that were on the curly side. "You're only thirty-two, hardly a senior citizen. And you have a nice figure. You look great."

Maybe. The red and black velvet dress was short, the flouncy skirt only coming to mid-thigh. Barely. The bodice was low-cut and what little cleavage I possessed had been corralled into a pushup bra that would have made Victoria proud. Luckily, Missy had also made a gorgeous red velvet hooded cloak that would at the very least make sure that I wasn't showing off too much of my rear assets. A wicker basket covered in a red silk scarf finished off the costume. That basket would come in handy tonight, carrying my phone and maybe a snack.

"It's so…short."

"You have terrific legs," Missy assured me with a wave of her hand. "Besides, you don't have any choice but to wear it. It's the only thing you have."

That wasn't exactly true. I had costumes from previous years stored away in the attic. I could dig them out but Missy knew I didn't have time. The guests were already beginning to arrive and I could hear the local band playing their first set of the evening.

Missy looked into the mirror to adjust her halo. She was dressed as an angel. She even had a harp, which was sitting on the bed next to my basket. "I bet the sheriff is going to like your costume."

Not again. The town seemed to hate the idea that I was happily unattached. They'd been throwing single men at me for the last four years and I'd been ducking them like an adolescent kid playing dodgeball.

"Do you think he'll want to borrow it for himself next year? He's a little tall for it."

"You know what I mean. Don't you think he's handsome?"

I shrugged, tightening the tie on my cloak. "Sure, I guess. I don't think about him any more than I have to. He's annoying, but even if he wasn't I'm not looking for a man in my life. Been there, done that. I'm never getting married again."

Missy sighed loudly. She'd been dating the same guy for almost three years. Eventually they were probably going to get married but they didn't seem to be any hurry. "You always say that."

"Because no one seems to be listening."

"You might change your mind."

"You might actually sprout real wings and fly, but what are the odds?"

Her brow lifted and smiled played around her lips. "Better than you might think. All I know is if I ever meet your ex-husband face to face I'm going to kick him where it counts."

"I'll be there to cheer you on."

My ex David was a handsome man just a year older than myself. We hit it off immediately and a year later tied the knot in a small ceremony in my parents' backyard. David didn't like to make a big deal of things and I had never wanted a big wedding anyway.

I thought we were doing okay – not great but okay – until I came home from Beelzebub and Co. and David was packing his bags. He'd said he wanted to find himself, an activity that I wholeheartedly supported since if something or someone is lost, you should definitely go find it. Or him. Or whatever.

Later I would find out that he basically wanted to find himself in the bed of as many different women as possible. I wholeheartedly supported that also as long as he wasn't my husband when he did it. As soon as the divorce was final, we sold the condo and split the proceeds. I immediately quit the job that I hated and moved back to Ravenmist. The inn had been limping along for a year with no clear management and I knew that's not what my grandmother would have wanted. My parents were thrilled that I wanted to take it over as they didn't have the time or inclination to run it.

Through all of this, Missy stood by my side drying my tears and telling me it would all get better. She was right. It did. And now she wanted me to do it all over again. Not going to happen.

I checked my reflection once more, smoothing down my flyaway hair before retrieving the last piece of my costume. The basket, now sitting by itself on the mattress. "I need to get out there. Where's your harp?"

My room wasn't that large and it only took a second to find it. The tiny plastic harp she'd purchased online now leaned against the wall near the window where a lovely autumn breeze was blowing into my bedroom. I had almost half of the downstairs as my living quarters. It wasn't huge but it was fine for me.

"Did you…?" I eyed the harp, moving my gaze from the bed to the where it now resided. Strange things were always happening in Ravenmist. I'd grown used to it long ago. "Never mind."

I walked over to the window to grab the harp for her and stopped when I saw Jerome Bergstrom in the distance wearing a Ghostbuster costume and talking to Roger, who was dressed as Henry the VIII. I couldn't hear what they were saying but visually they both appeared to be upset. Jerome was waving his arms in the air and Roger kept trying to walk away, only to have Jerome follow him.

"What are you looking at?"

Missy had come up behind me, also peering out of the window. "I saw that Ghostbuster arguing with some man in Daisy's at lunchtime. Looks like he has people issues."

Daisy owned the local cafe and she was quite the character. Remind me to introduce you.

"Was it that man? His name is Roger."

Missy shook her head. "No, it was someone else. A few years older and heavier."

"What were they arguing about?"

Roger disappeared around the corner of the inn with Jerome on his heels.

"I'm not sure. I was only in there to pick up some food and take it back to the store. I heard the Ghostbuster say something like *you can't do that to me* and the other guy said *yes, I can.*

Other than that, I don't know. They were mad, though. Their faces were bright red and all the other diners were uncomfortable."

Jerome appeared to have issues with more than just his wife Lorna. He really should think about the way he interacted with others. My grandmother Rose used to say that a person could catch more flies with honey than vinegar.

Pushing Jerome and his anger management problems out of my head, I reached for the harp on the floor but it wasn't there.

"Wait...wasn't it...?"

I turned to quickly scan the room and the harp sat on the bed. Six feet away from where I'd last seen it.

"Did you move it, Missy? Because I didn't see you do it."

She picked up the tiny harp and laughed. "Of course, I did. You don't think ghosts did it, do you?"

In this town, one could never tell.

"Are you ready to go have some fun?" Missy grinned and ran her fingers over the plastic strings, making a discordant sound that reminded me of an angry cat falling in the water. "It's the highlight of the year for Ravenmist. Let's go request that the band play 'Monster Mash'. Maybe the sheriff will ask you to dance."

I checked the window again but I didn't see any flying pigs in the sky. Nope, I wasn't going to be doing any dancing with Jackson Garrett.

Chapter Three

THE PARTY WAS in full swing and everyone was having a wonderful time. The decorations looked even better at night with all the spooky lights and the draped spiderwebs hanging from the trees. Strategically placed mist machines spewed gray fog over the ground, adding to the ghostly vibe.

The branches, leaves and lights made a canopy over the path to the garden, and that's where I was headed to make sure that no one had bashed in anyone's skull with a sledgehammer. If that happened I was sure that Garrett would never let me hear the end of it.

I was alone on the trail and I paused for a moment when I saw a gray, misty figure in the distance. As the head ghost hunter in our local paranormal society I froze, not moving a muscle. If this was an actual ghost sighting that meant I had now seen…let me count…hmmmm…

If this was a real spirit then I would have seen *one* ghost in my life. One.

Okay, I know what you're thinking and I don't blame you. I must really suck as a ghost hunter if I've never actually seen one.

Ravenmist is definitely haunted. I've known that my whole life. I'd grown up listening to stories at my grandmother's knee. Even my dad, who was normally as straight-laced and sober as any man could be, had stories of the strange things that had happened in town. He swears to this day that he had a ghost-child best friend for a few years when he was a kid. Both my grandparents had seen ghosts, as have many of the townsfolk throughout the years, although the sightings seem to have dried up in the internet age.

Maybe spirits don't like social media. Can't say that I blame them.

So just because I personally hadn't witnessed a ghost didn't mean that there weren't any in Ravenmist. Weird stuff was always happening and there wasn't always a logical explanation.

The sound of a snapping twig from behind me had me whirling around, only to come face to face with Garrett and his son Tyler. Tyler was dressed as a vampire, complete with black cape and fangs. Garrett was dressed in his sheriff's uniform. Honestly, he couldn't cut loose just one night?

I quickly turned back to where I'd seen the gray figure but it was now gone, thanks to our friendly law enforcement officer.

"Sheriff," I said through gritted teeth. "You scared away what might have been a full-body apparition."

Garrett hooked his thumbs in his belt and quirked a brow. "A full body apparition? You mean a ghost? Why would a ghost be scared of me and Tyler? Doesn't make sense, does it? Kind of like ghosts and goblins in general."

I'd had it with this man. He thought he was so smart and all of us here in Ravenmist were just country bumpkins. I'd met so many like him when I'd worked in Chicago.

"I never said I believed in goblins but I know what I saw."

Pursing his lips, Garrett regarded the long path. "Down there, you mean? Is that where you saw it? Are you sure you don't have a ghost confused with the mist machine? The wind is pushing that stuff all over the place. It's dangerous. Someone could trip over a tree stump and hurt themselves."

He was such a pessimist. He saw danger and mayhem everywhere.

"I know a ghost from mist."

Tyler, who was fifteen, had already taken off down the path and had to be called back by his dad.

"There's nothing there, son. It's just mist."

Ignoring his father, Tyler turned to me. "Have you seen a lot of ghosts?"

Garrett grinned and crossed his arms over his chest. "That's a great question, Ty. Have you seen many ghosts, Ms. Hamilton?"

I gave the sheriff my best stink eye. "I haven't, but I've heard stories since the day I was born. Ravenmist is haunted and it's only a matter of time before you realize that, too. Even if you never actually see a ghost, you'll see their handiwork. Lots of strange going-ons here in town."

"The strangest thing I've seen is you traipsing around in the dark after a ghost made of mist."

I wanted to slap that smirk off of his face, but I could tell that Tyler was watching our back and forth with great interest. I wasn't going to set a bad example for the young man.

"Back at you, Sheriff. You stick out like a sore thumb in Ravenmist."

"I'll take that as a compliment. Were you headed to the garden? I was going there to check on how many people had been beaned with that sledgehammer so far."

My jaw ached from holding in the blistering words I wanted to send his way. Being nasty, however, wasn't what a lady did. Just ask my mother, Peggy Evans Hamilton. She'll tell you. Over and over again. Whether you want her to or not.

Speaking of my mother...where was she? She and dad never missed a festival. Last year they'd dressed as Romeo and Juliet. They'd been married forever and were the most nauseatingly happy couple I'd ever seen. Their couple costumes were legendary and looked forward to every year.

"Yes, I'm headed to the garden."

Tyler was a typical teenager and I could tell hanging out with his dad wasn't his choice. He was wearing a bored expression and the only time he'd perked up was when I'd mentioned the ghost. Garrett had probably dragged him around all evening. With me here, the kid saw an out. I didn't blame him.

"Hey Dad, since you two are going to check on the game do you mind if I go grab some food? I'm starving."

"We were going to do that after this."

"I'm hungry now. You can catch up with me." Tyler rolled his eyes to the sky like only a teenager could do. "I'll be right near the buffet. What trouble can I get into?"

"With you, I never know. Okay, but you go to the buffet and stay there. This should only take a few minutes."

Tyler was fifteen freakin' years old. At that age, I was running around Ravenmist and I doubt my parents had any idea where I was most of the time.

The teenager didn't hesitate when his dad gave the okay, turning and sprinting back up the path, his cape waving in the wind behind him like a superhero.

"You know, Ravenmist has almost no crime whatsoever. I grew up here and even when I wanted to get into mischief there was none to be had. It quite possibly is the most boring place to grow up in the entire world."

For the first time since I'd met Jackson Garrett, he didn't look like he had all the answers. He actually looked kind of sad. "If there's trouble, Tyler can find it. That's a big reason why I moved here."

I hadn't known that and I kind of felt bad for Garrett. Sort of. If he hadn't wanted to leave Chicago this change had to be tough on him.

"The rumor around town is that your leaving Chicago has something to do with an injury."

I didn't mention the slight limp he walked with. It was barely noticeable and not a big deal.

The sheriff slapped his right thigh. "They would be right. I was shot and they wanted me to ride a desk. That coupled with the bad crowd Tyler had fallen in with made the decision to leave easy. I wanted to bring him to a place that didn't have any bad influences."

Did such a place exist? I doubted it. And then one had to assume that Tyler Garrett hadn't been the actual bad influence back in Chicago. He looked like a pretty good kid, though.

"So you brought him to a haunted town. Interesting."

Garrett shook his head and started down the path. "No, I brought him to a safe little town that people like to say is haunted because it brings in tourists. There's a big difference."

I headed off after him, his long legs going far faster than my usual stride. I had to jog to keep up with him. "You haven't been here long enough. You'll see."

"I don't care to see–"

He stopped and I ran into him, my nose meeting the middle of his back and knocking me sideways a few steps. He reached out to steady me and then placed a finger over my lips to keep me quiet before pointing to my right. I turned and saw good old Jerome Bergstrom in a clinch with a woman who clearly was not his wife. In fact, I knew the woman. She was Angela Warner, a real estate agent here in Ravenmist. I'd gone to high school with her, although she was a few years ahead of me.

I brushed Garrett's fingers away but didn't speak as Jerome and Angela kissed passionately in the shroud of darkness off of the path. The only reason we could even see them tonight was the full moon overhead. Any other night they would have been undetected.

Garrett's fingers wrapped around my arm and gently urged

me down the path toward the garden. We didn't say anything for a few minutes until the happy sounds and bright lights of the party could be seen or heard. I paused at the edge of the hay bale maze, guests milling around us.

"That was one of my guests with Angela Warner. I wonder if she knows he's married with kids."

Shaking his head, Garrett's lips were pressed together grimly. "It's none of our business, Tedi. Don't go there. Trust me on this. I know small towns like to gossip but I can assure you nothing good would come from it, nor would it be welcomed should you decide to let her know. We need to stay out of this."

"I wasn't suggesting I wanted to get involved. I have no intention of doing so, either. I was just making an observation."

"I don't think any part of that was meant to be observed. Just forget you saw it. Take my advice…never get involved in anyone else's marriage."

It had been bad enough to be in my own.

"As I said before, I wasn't planning to do anything. Now are we going to check the games? I guarantee you no one has been hurt."

Except for Lorna Bergstrom. And maybe Jerome, if his wife ever caught him. He was a man playing with fire.

As THE OWNER of an inn, I was used to waking up early. I wasn't the happiest person in those moments before the sun came up but it was part of the job. Waking up the morning after a party when I'd barely had three hours of sleep wasn't a piece of cake, either. I couldn't go to bed until the very last guest left. That had been three-thirty in the morning and it was currently six. I normally got out of bed a half hour earlier but I was reasonably sure that my guests wouldn't be up and wanting breakfast at the crack of dawn.

If anything, they'd be wanting hot black coffee and some Alka-Seltzer. Maybe a puke bucket, too.

Ravenmist knew how to throw a party and it had been quite the success. I'd lost track of how many cases of booze we'd run through and the band had been on fire. They'd played until two in the morning. Yes, it had taken an hour and a half to shoo everyone back to their homes or hotel rooms.

I'd slipped on my favorite, soft as butter ripped blue jeans and a University of Illinois sweatshirt, my feet stuffed in a pair of worn tennis shoes. They were butt ugly and held together by dirt and prayer but they were so gosh darn comfortable. I shoved my nose close to the coffeemaker as it dripped into the pot, dark and steamy. It smelled like heaven and I took a big whiff, filling my lungs with its French roast goodness.

Pouring myself a cup, I dumped some cream and sugar in it before wandering through the house. It was a disaster area as I hadn't bothered to clean up after the guests left. My staff had been fantastic and wrapped up all the food, stowing it in the massive refrigerator. I would put it all out around midday for anyone that felt well enough to venture out of their room.

There were paper cups and plates strewn all over, orange and black balloons drifting through the living room and hallways, and random pieces of costumes tossed aside. A set of devil horns here, a fake mustache there. My lips quirked as I picked up a pile of white netting that turned out to be a tutu for a toddler.

The sun was just beginning to rise over the horizon and I opened the French doors that connected the living room to the expansive back patio. The air was crisp and I was glad I'd chosen a sweatshirt this morning. Goosebumps rose on my arms and I took another sip of hot coffee. What a glorious day it was going to be. Sunny and absolutely perfect.

The patio tables were no less a mess and I mentally calculated how long it would take to set the inn to rights. This wasn't my first year doing it and I had a system now. I wished I'd paid more attention when my grandmother was alive and running the inn but back then I'd never thought I would be here. When I was young all I wanted to do was get out of Ravenmist. Now I never wanted to leave, unless it was for a vacation or maybe a quick shopping trip into the city to get their famous pizza.

A set of orange and black helium balloons were whipping in the wind and I didn't want them to float away. I'd read articles about how terrible balloons were for animal life and the environment. I thought that I'd brought all of them in last night but obviously I'd missed a few.

I managed to untie them from the railing and turned to head into the house when my gaze landed on the apple bobbing tub a few feet away. I blinked a few times and shook my head, not sure exactly what I was seeing. The sun, however, was now higher in the sky and the image was unmistakable.

A man. Face down in the tub full of apples and water, a knife protruding from his back up near the neck. An arm hung down with the same gold watch wrapped around its wrist that I'd seen yesterday.

There were no bubbles on the surface of the water to indicate that he was still breathing.

Heavens to Betsy, Jerome Bergstrom was dead.

Chapter Four

EVERY PERSON IN Ravenmist must have heard the news because there were people everywhere I looked, stuffed into every corner of the inn and grounds. Garrett had taped off the area with yellow crime scene tape and the county coroner had pulled the body from the water.

Note to self. Stabbing and drowning is not a pretty way to die.

Second note to self. Jackson Garrett took murder very seriously.

He was currently wearing a grim expression and growling at two of his deputies, who both looked extremely hungover. The family and friends of Jerome Bergstrom had been cordoned off in my drawing room with a third deputy guarding that door. He looked hungover too, his skin tinged green as if any minute he was going to boot up the contents of his stomach. I'd placed a garbage can close by just in case. The last thing I needed was for him to sully the antique umbrella stand in the corner. It was over a hundred years old.

I was trying to be everywhere at once, organizing food for the police and the coroner, plus all the guests who were now wide awake and curious about what had happened. They'd expected ghosts and got a dead body instead.

This probably wasn't going to be good for business.

I was also trying to assure my guests that this wasn't a usual occurrence in Ravenmist. In fact, I couldn't remember the last murder in our little town. Maybe when I was a child? In other words, they had nothing to fear.

Missy had arrived at some point along with my parents, who had been a no-show last night. I was still wondering about that and the minute I had time to take a breath I was planning to ask them what had happened. I couldn't remember a time when they'd missed the festival. I hoped they weren't ill.

Garrett pulled me aside as I was directing one of my kitchen staff to serve the leftover food buffet style. My mother was waving at me to get my attention but the sheriff was determined to talk to me first.

"I need your official statement."

Missy was now talking to my parents and leading them to the food. That should keep them busy for a few minutes.

"I gave you my statement already. I'm not going to change it."

Garrett rubbed at his chin. "You said you came out here and found him face down in the washtub filled with water and apples."

"That's correct."

"And?"

Not sure what he wanted me to say and really not liking his tone, I crossed my arms over my chest protectively. "And what? That's what happened. I saw his body and ran back into the inn to call you."

"And you didn't touch or move the body?"

I shuddered at the thought. "Um...no."

"But when you called you said it Jerome Bergstrom. How did you know?"

That was what this was about? He needed to stop playing "Columbo".

"I saw that gold watch on his wrist. He was wearing it when he checked in yesterday. It wasn't hard to recognize."

"Someone else could have one like it."

My lips twisted and I shook my head. "I doubt it. It was certainly...one of a kind and not in a good way."

It was butt-ugly. Was he going to make me say it out loud?

"And while you were waiting for me to get here you informed Mrs. Bergstrom about her husband?"

"No."

"She was downstairs when I got here. Did one of the staff alert her?"

I huffed, slightly impatient with all the questions. I'd only found the body. I didn't know who killed the poor man. Did I have to do all of the work for the sheriff?

"I doubt it, although it's possible. I was pretty much the only one awake and then a few kitchen staff showed up. I guess they could have after I told them to stay out of the backyard. I didn't want to contaminate your crime scene, Sheriff."

I'd watched all the reruns of "Sherlock" on Netflix at least twice.

"I appreciate that, Tedi, although I'm not sure it's doing any good now. Is all of Ravenmist here?"

"It's a small town. Word travels fast."

He flipped a page in his little notebook where he was making notes. "In Chicago I didn't have an audience."

"I should have sold tickets. Now am I done?"

"One more question. What were you doing out here in the first place?"

Sighing heavily, I looked around for my cup. "I was having some coffee – which seems to have disappeared – and I stepped outside to watch the sunrise and see how much cleaning we had ahead of us today. Nothing nefarious, I can assure you."

Grimacing, he nodded toward the horde of people milling in my inn and on my lawn. "I don't think you're going to get much done today. They're only making it worse. I will keep them off this side of the patio though, and that means your staff as well. That's my crime scene."

It was my inn but I was okay letting him borrow part of it for awhile. I wouldn't be visiting that particular area of the back patio for a long time without seeing Jerome Bergstrom slumped over in the apple tub with a knife in his back.

"Do you know who did it yet?"

Lifting his arm, Garrett checked his watch. "Considering I've been here less than two hours, the answer would be no. Shockingly, not one person has run up to me and confessed, either. Why? Do you know who did it? You said you didn't see anyone."

I held up my hands in surrender. Touchy, wasn't he? "I didn't see anyone. This entire area was deserted. I was just asking. You've been asking lots of questions. I thought you might have a few answers by now."

He nodded toward the inn. "The most important questions are still to be asked. I need to speak to Lorna Bergstrom."

The wife. Statistically speaking, the most likely suspect. At least that's what I'd seen on television. Plus, she'd wished she'd never married the dearly departed Jerome. That would be an interesting conversation. Too bad I wouldn't be allowed to listen.

Or would I? My closet was on the other side of the wall of the drawing room where Lorna Bergstrom was currently waiting.

I REALLY NEEDED to clean out my closet.

Deep in the recesses of the small space, I had shoved my old corporate America clothes along with my wedding dress that I kept saying I needed to sell on eBay. Or burn in a backyard sacrifice to the gods of barbecue chicken and potato salad. I really wasn't fussy about how it exited my life. It had been hideously expensive for something so simple but that was a little tidbit I'd learned when shopping for the infernal thing. The simpler the dress, the more it cost.

Shoving past a wool winter coat, I tripped over a pair of high heeled brown boots. Muffling the four-letter word that instantly came to my lips, I rubbed my knee that had come in contact a pair of red pumps that looked amazing with a little black dress. The box with my veil, shoes, and petticoat should have also been in my way but instead it was pushed to the side and propped against the hanging clothes. I didn't remember moving it, but then weird stuff was always happening and I really never knew where any item was going to be located. I'd grown used to it over the years and this time it was just lucky. I was able to wedge right next to the wall.

There was no need for a glass like in the movies or to press my ear to the wall. This house was old and there had been a fair amount of renovations and additions to the home. This section of the house had been an add-on and the person who had done the construction hadn't bothered to take out the window to the outside, simply leaving it in the wall of my closet.

Knowing my grandmother, she hadn't thought it was a big deal since it was only a place to hang one's clothes. She'd placed a heavy drape over it on the wardrobe side and probably forgotten all about it. It looked quite decorative from the drawing room. Few people had any idea that my walk-in closet was on the other side.

It was that red velvet drape that I lifted ever so slightly so I could hear what was being said. Just a few inches. I couldn't see what was going on but I should be able to listen with no problem.

Right now, several people were talking, all trying to be heard and I couldn't make out what they were saying. Finally, a man cleared his throat – it had to be Garrett – and everyone quieted down.

"Take your time, Mrs. Bergstrom. No detail is too small. What happened after you and your husband left the party?"

There was a sniffle or two. Probably Lorna, although it might be the friends.

"I've just lost my husband. Can't this wait?"

"I'm afraid not. There are a few hundred tourists in town and they could leave at any moment. One of them might have done this."

"Then tell them not to leave."

Right. Like Garrett could physically stop them. I had to stifle a giggle at the image of him lying down on the road to block their escape.

"I have, but legally I can't force them to stay, ma'am. If you want me to find your husband's killer, I need you to help me."

"Lorna, the sheriff needs your help. What do you remember?"

That was a woman's voice. It must be Cherie Mullaney.

"There was nothing out of the ordinary. We went up to the room together and got ready for bed. He talked about a business meeting he had in the city on Monday morning. Then we fell asleep. When I woke up he was gone. I assumed he was downstairs getting coffee and a newspaper, but then one of the maids knocked on the door and told me that there had been a murder downstairs."

"What did you do then?"

That was Garrett again.

"I threw on some clothes and ran downstairs."

"No, you knocked on our door on the way." Another masculine voice. Roger Mullaney. "And we went downstairs with you."

"Yes, that's right." Lorna Bergstrom sounded as if she was out of breath and had run a marathon. "Of course, I stopped and got you two first and then we went downstairs."

Or not. Lorna didn't sound too darn sure about that. It was a simple detail and she'd missed it. Did that impugn all of her statement? I wasn't sure, but I personally wasn't feeling the truth vibe from the older woman.

Garrett wasn't done. "You didn't wake up when your husband got out of bed? Is that usual for you?"

"Jerry works until all hours. I'm used to him coming to bed late and getting up early. But last night I took a little sleeping pill to help me get some rest. I don't sleep well away from my own bed."

Everyone was different, but I always woke up when my louse of an ex got out of bed. He wasn't an early bird but he did suffer from insomnia, and when I say suffer that means I did right along with him. When he couldn't sleep he didn't want anyone else to sleep, either. If I wouldn't entertain him, then he'd call up a friend whether it was two in the morning or two in the afternoon.

"That's very convenient, ma'am. Do you have a prescription?"

You tell 'em, Sheriff. It was a trifle too convenient to have slept through the entire murder.

"They're mine, Sheriff." Cherie's voice. "I loaned one to Lorna when she said she was going to have trouble sleeping. I can get the bottle for you if you'd like to see what they are."

"Yes, please. One of my deputies will escort you."

"Oh, that's not necessary. I know the way."

"Actually…it is."

There was silence and I wished I could see their expressions. Cherie must have decided not to say anything because I heard a door open and close along with some footsteps. She must be headed to her room.

"I hope you don't think any of us did this, Sheriff. We've been friends with Jerry and Lorna for years."

Roger's voice. He sounded shocked, which was crazy. Didn't he watch any mysteries? Close friends and family were always suspects.

"Right now, I haven't ruled anyone out. What were you doing early this morning, Mr. Mullaney?"

"Now see here, I won't be talked to this way. I'll call a lawyer."

"If you feel that you need an attorney, then you should call one. I'm going to need Mrs. Mullaney's whereabouts as well."

I heard a huff of exasperation before the reply. "She was asleep. Next to me all night."

"Were you asleep?"

"Of course."

"Then how can you know for sure?"

"Lorna, I'd advise you not to answer any more questions until we get Byron down here," Roger said with another huff. If he wasn't careful he was going to hyperventilate. "The sheriff doesn't have any suspects or clues and he clearly needs to pin this on someone."

I wasn't a fan of Jackson Garrett but he didn't seem the type, although I'd been fooled before. I prided myself, however, on not being fooled twice.

"I'm going to run this investigation as fairly as possible, Mr. Mullaney, and that means treating everyone equally until they are ruled out as suspects."

"I was in my room. Surely this inn has security cameras? Pull the footage and you'll see."

What did he think this place was? The Marriott? It was a two-hundred-year-old inn that had last been rewired in the eighties before the internet and Wi-Fi.

Located in the safest town in America.

"I'll find Tedi right now and ask her."

Garrett better not find me on the other side of the wall. I dropped the heavy drape and as quietly as I could and crept out of the closet and into my bedroom. Checking my reflection in the mirror, I smoothed down my hair. Time to give them the bad news.

They'd have to find another way to prove their innocence.

Chapter Five

WHEN I LEFT my apartment Garrett wasn't anywhere around, which was a relief. I'd have to deal with him eventually but the later the better, as far as I was concerned. I headed straight to the kitchen to check on how the leftovers were holding out and also if they'd started dinner preparation. The inn wasn't going to do a lunch service today because of the festival and I wasn't planning on feeding the entire town, either. Once the food from the festival was gone, it was gone. Most of the townsfolk would wander away when the free eats disappeared, although a few diehards would hang around. They weren't here for the food but the murder.

The kitchen was bustling with activity, but it was the man and woman sitting at the huge kitchen island that caught my attention. My wayward parents who hadn't shown up last night. I'd assumed one of them was hospitalized or on their deathbed with malaria or some flesh-eating disease.

"Mom. Dad. I've been worried about you. Did you get my messages?"

I'd left several but not past nine-thirty. My parents – Dan

and Peggy Hamilton – liked to turn in early and if they weren't feeling well I didn't want to disturb their sleep. They looked, however, healthy as could be with pink cheeks and big smiles. My dad's once blond hair had turned gray but his blue eyes still twinkled with life and energy. My mother was an older version of me, right down to the auburn hair and brown eyes. Both of them currently had a plate of food so they weren't fighting a bout of stomach flu.

Peggy and Dan exchanged a glance before my mother patted the bar stool next to her. "Come join us, dear. We're having a bite to eat."

I slid into the seat next to my mother and pinched a piece of brownie from her plate. "Seriously, I was worried about you last night. You never miss the festival. It's a tradition."

Another glance between them. Something fishy was going on. Had Aunt Hattie escaped from the senior center again and gone on the run? Last time it had taken ten days to find her shacked up with a Hell's Angel.

Did I mention that my family could be described as *colorful* and *entertaining*? At least my mom's side.

Dan cleared his throat and placed his napkin beside his plate. "Actually, sweetheart, we were worried about you after we heard the news. This is just awful."

My mom nodded vigorously, casting a glance over her shoulder at the kitchen staff before leaning closer to speak. "Do you think this will hurt business?"

I'd thought about that quite a bit in the past few hours and come to a conclusion.

"I don't think so. We already have a reputation as a haunted hotel. I think we'll be fine." They weren't going to sidetrack me. "You still didn't say what happened to you last night."

Peggy put her hand on mine and gave it a squeeze. "There's a few things we've been meaning to tell you."

I knew it.

"This is about Aunt Hattie, isn't it? Has she been arrested? Or is she missing? Have they checked the taverns within a hundred-mile radius?"

My dad's brows shot up and he shook his head. "No, pumpkin. This isn't about Aunt Hattie. It's…well…I'm not sure how to say this."

My heart froze and I laid a hand on my chest, sure I was not going to hear a heartbeat. I was wrong. It was beating but far too fast.

"Are you…sick?" I was afraid to even put my worst fears into words. "Oh my God, is one of you dying?"

"Dying?" Mom echoed, her guileless brown eyes wide. "You think we're dying?"

I hopped up from the barstool and began to pace the small space, the words tumbling out quickly one after the other. I don't remember the last time I was this scared. "What else am I to think? You're acting all strange and this isn't about our relatives. One of you must be sick. Which one of you is it? We'll get the best doctors. I still have friends in Chicago and they know people at Northwestern University. We'll get you into a medical trial. I have savings, too. We can fly you out of the country for treatment if we have to."

Jumping up from his own chair, my father came around to stop my pacing, placing his hands on my shoulders and holding me still. "Pumpkin, we're not dying. We're not sick."

I was so frustrated I couldn't even be relieved.

"Then what is going on that you don't want to tell me? And don't lie, because I can see that there is something wrong. What is it?"

Dad looked at Mom and she sighed. "Your father and I are getting a divorce."

My gaze darted back and forth between them but they didn't appear to be joking. Just in case I waited before replying, hoping that my dad might break into laughter and tell me it was only a prank. A tasteless one, but a prank nonetheless. Nothing like a good scare so close to Halloween.

My mind was having a hard time wrapping around my mother's statement, though. A divorce. They'd been married forty-one years at this point. Were they indecisive? I knew pretty quickly that I'd made a mistake. It didn't take me forty freakin' years to figure it out.

Oh God. What if one of them was having an affair? Eww.

"A divorce?"

It seemed safer to simply parrot what they were saying and hope they would explain.

Dad nodded, his arms falling to his sides. "We've been want-ing to tell you for a long time but we didn't know how to do it."

A long time?

"How long?"

Mom fidgeted on her barstool. "Awhile. A few months. Your dad moved into the space over the garage right after the Fourth."

How had I never noticed this? I saw these people practically on a daily basis.

"Of July?" I asked, my voice getting louder. The kitchen staff came to a halt and a quiet spread over the kitchen. That's when I realized we had an audience. I turned to the cooks and mustered what I hoped was a smile. "How about everyone take a little break? Get some fresh air. I need to speak with my parents."

Sitting heavily back onto the barstool I waited until all of the kitchen staff had shuffled out, leaving me alone with the two people who had raised me. That right now I wanted to smack some sense into.

"You cannot get a divorce," I said once we were alone in the kitchen. "You've been married forever. You're…old."

I didn't mean it to come out quite like that but…they weren't twenty-two anymore. At their age, they had to be slowing down, if only a little bit. I was in my early thirties and half the time felt like I was seventy.

Slapping her cup down on the island, Peggy's lips flattened into a line. "I am not that old, young lady, and I'm certainly not too old to turn you over my knee. When you're my age you won't think you're old."

I imagine being old is a little like being crazy. You're the last one to know you are. So my parents were having some sort of late mid-life crisis. That was normal, right? People all over the world were doing this. Probably.

"Fine, you're young." A thought occurred to me. "But you are definitely too old to spank me. That is so not going to happen."

"Then I'll send you to your room."

That wasn't exactly a punishment.

My father cleared his throat again. "What we're trying to tell you is that we've separated and are planning to divorce. I'll be moving out in a few days so we knew we had to tell you now."

My vision blurred for a moment and the room spun before righting itself. "Moving out? You're moving out. Listen, every marriage has issues but you have to work on them. See a counselor. Go on a second honeymoon. Buy a Harley. It worked for Aunt Hattie."

My mother shrugged and fiddled with her fork. "We've done all of that. Except for the motorcycle, of course. It didn't help. We don't have forever on this planet and we want a chance to be happy."

I was still floored from hearing that they'd seen a marriage counselor but then I thought about my sisters. They were going to be extremely upset, especially Amelia. She cried at the drop of a hat. She even cried when she thought something bad *might* happen. Sort of a preemptive sob session.

Rubbing my temples, I tried to slow my racing heart by slowly inhaling and then exhaling. My parents were being impetuous, which wasn't like them at all. Well…it wasn't like my father.

That was it. This was my mother's idea. It had her finger-prints all over it and Daddy was just going along with it to make her happy. Like he always did. He was simply humoring her and eventually it would all go back to the way it was.

"When are you going to tell the others?"

Another guilty glance. I was hating this day more and more. They had to tell my sisters.

My dad shifted on his feet, looking everywhere but directly at me. He finally lifted his gaze, apology written all over his features. "We already have, pumpkin. A few months ago."

A few months ago.

The words echoed in my brain and I heard them over and over but I couldn't quite comprehend their meaning.

"I don't understand."

"We told them when they were in town for my birthday in August," Mom said, her chin lifted as if to dare me to complain about it. She'd also practically dared me not to go to Chicago and look how that turned out.

"You told them but not me? Am I getting this right?"

I realized my mouth was hanging open in shock and that I was feeling angry. Very angry. I loved my parents but that didn't mean that they couldn't honk me off at times.

"It's just...you're so emotional," my mother sighed. "And we didn't want to bring back the memory of your own divorce. This is nothing like that. We're happy about this and we're still friends."

Oh no, they just didn't...

"Don't turn this around on me," I said, my voice quivering with emotion and just plain hurt. "This is about you two being too chicken-livered to tell me. All my sisters have flown the coop and don't have to deal with it day in and day out so it was easy to tell them. But me? Nope. You waited until the last minute. I have to give props though, my loving parents. You told me on the perfect day. I'm just sorry your news was eclipsed by some poor dead guy."

Dad reached out for me but I dodged his hand. I was in no mood to deal with this.

"I have an inn to run and a murder to deal with. But hey, thanks for making my day even better. Have a great divorce. Will you let me know if you're getting married to anyone again or will I have to read that in the paper like everyone else? I guess I can just ask my sisters." I began to walk away and but then stopped and turned around. "And I am not the emotional one. Amelia is."

Before they could reply I stomped out of the kitchen, a righteous head of steam built up. What a horrible day and yet I didn't have much to complain about. Jerome Bergstrom was having a much worse day. Had Garrett found the killer yet?

Chapter Six

SHERIFF JACKSON GARRETT was on my last nerve.

"Are you crazy? Have you lost your mind? Missy didn't do anything wrong."

Garrett sighed and I could see a muscle jerk in his jaw. He was mad. Too bad, so was I. Between a dead body on my back lawn and my parents splitting up I'd had the day from hell.

"She was seen walking toward your backyard, Tedi, by a credible witness. Your own paper boy. Why would he lie?"

"I have a better question. Why would Missy kill a guy she's never met?" I shot back. "It doesn't make any sense and you have to admit that. She has no motive whatsoever while there are others who have lots of motive. Tons of it. Besides, he could have been mistaken. It was dark and he could have seen someone that just looked like Missy."

I was ready to argue with Garrett until my last breath if I had to. He appeared to be gearing up to do the same until we both heard a voice behind us.

"It was me. He wasn't mistaken."

Whirling around, I saw Missy standing there in my personal

living room where I'd dragged the sheriff when he started in on wanting to speak to her. I didn't need the staff and half of the town gossiping about something that wasn't even true.

Except that it was and it didn't make any sense at all.

"What were you doing out at that hour?" I asked, ignoring my law enforcement nemesis. "Is everything okay? Were you coming to see me?"

Missy nodded and closed the door behind her, stifling the noises from the inn. The food had officially run out but people were still milling about. "I was and then I realized that it was ridiculous to come over at that time of the morning. I'm sorry but I was just upset."

"Upset about what?"

This time Garrett beat me to the punch and asked his question first.

"That's kind of personal isn't it?" I asked testily. "It's none of your business. She gave you the reason she was out and about and now you need to leave her alone."

"There is nothing private in a murder investigation. So I'll ask the question again. Miss Harper, what were you so upset about that you needed to come over before five in the morning, walking in the dark?"

I rolled my eyes at his hyperbole. "This is Ravenmist, Sheriff. Nothing is going to happen to her in the dark or the light. We don't even have a bad part of town."

The sound of Garrett's pencil hitting his notepad sounded loud in my ears. He was ticked.

"First of all, you most certainly do have a bad part of town. The old downtown is none too safe."

"It's not dangerous. It's haunted."

"Have you ever found a ghost there?"

I couldn't believe that the town thought he was attractive. All he needed was a mustache to twirl and he could be a real live villain in an old silent movie.

"Not yet."

"Well, I found some vagrants so I win." He turned back to Missy, turning his back on me. "Miss Harper? Could you answer the question, please?"

"My boyfriend and I had a big argument. He's talking about leaving town to take a new job and he wants me to go with him."

This was the first I was hearing of this. Dylan and Missy were very happy together. At no time had I ever heard him expressing interest in leaving Ravenmist. His family had lived here for four generations and ran the feed store in town. What kind of job was he going to take?

"Are you going?"

Of all the questions I could have asked it wasn't pertinent to getting Garrett off of my best friend's back, but it was the first one that came to mind. I didn't want to lose Missy. She was my rock in this town, especially now that my parents had officially lost their minds.

Missy smiled and shook her head. "No way. I'm here to stay."

Turning on Garrett, I shrugged nonchalantly. "See? A perfectly reasonable explanation. Now you should go out and find the real killer before they leave town."

I must have said something funny because the sheriff chuckled. "You're so sure that no Ravenmist citizen did this?"

"No one knew Jerome Bergstrom."

That's when it hit me. Angela Warner knew him.

"Miss Harper, don't leave town. I may need to speak to you again."

With her finger, Missy crossed her heart. "I'm not going anywhere. I didn't do anything wrong."

"Of course, you didn't. He must have lots of suspects other than you, right, Sheriff?"

I gave him my best mean look but he wasn't fazed in the least. I could picture him twirling that mustache.

"No."

"A few then?"

"No. Just one."

Then I'd find him some more. Garrett Jackson wasn't going to pin this murder on my best friend just because she'd had the bad luck to be walking around in the middle of the night. If he couldn't find who murdered Jerome Bergstrom then I would.

And I'd start with the girlfriend.

"I NEED A new house," I announced to Angela Warner as I sat

down in her guest chair. Her real estate office wasn't far from the inn and I'd walked there as soon as I could get away from Sheriff Jackass. Oops. I mean Sheriff Jackson Garrett. "I'm tired of living in the inn. It's like I'm always at work."

"Of course, I can help you," Angela said with a smile. She was an attractive woman with short dark hair and expressive green eyes. Right now, those eyes were looking at me with sympathy and I felt a twinge of guilt being here, but then I remembered she might be a murderer. "After today, I can imagine that you're looking for peace and quiet. A place you can go to retreat from your day to day stresses."

I wasn't for real looking for a house but that didn't sound too bad. Maybe I should seriously think about it. Because I lived in the inn I basically worked twenty-four hours a day, seven days a week. I loved the inn but a girl could only take so much, you know?

"You heard about Mr. Bergstrom?" I asked, my gaze sweeping around the office looking for...what? I didn't know. I wasn't a cop, after all. I'd been a research analyst at a financial firm in my previous corporate life but all that meant was that I had the patience to do limitless grunt work. "The whole situation is just shocking. I can't imagine why anyone would want him dead. He was so friendly and charming."

Hopefully lightning would be busy elsewhere since I'd just told a whopper of a lie. My hair didn't singe and the electricity didn't go off so I figured I was safe for now.

Angela leaned forward, a solemn look on her face. "It's awful. What is this world coming to? I mean, what is wrong with people? The poor man comes into town on vacation and ends up dead. It's shocking, that's what it is."

Leaning back in the chair, I casually crossed my legs hoping to look innocent and nonchalant, not like I was trying to find out any secrets she might have.

"Did you get a chance to meet him at the party last night?"

Not a flicker of a reaction. None.

"I'm afraid I wasn't at the party long. I stayed for less than and hour as I was a little under the weather."

"I hope you're feeling better today," I replied with the appropriate amount of concern in my tone. Angela Warner was a smooth liar and I kind of admired her for it. I, on the other hand, sucked at it. "I can come back another time…"

She waved away my concerns. "I'm fine. Don't worry about me. Now let's talk about what you're looking for in a house. Bedrooms, bathrooms, size of the yard. Will you want something close to the inn or are you looking to move farther out of town?"

"That's an excellent question." A deep voice boomed behind me and I closed my eyes, taking a deep breath. Jackson Garrett. So he did have other suspects. Turning around in my chair, I checked to see if his pants were on fire but surprisingly found them untouched. It appeared lightning and fire were occupied today. Lucky us. "I had no idea, Tedi, that you were planning to make a change in your living situation."

"The news will be in the paper next week," I replied with a saccharine smile. "I'm taking out an ad."

Angela's brows shot up at my tone and her gaze bounced back and forth between us. Clearly Garrett and I were more interesting than how many half baths I wanted.

"I'll look forward to it." Garrett nodded his head but there was a glint in his blue eyes. I was going to be hearing about this later. "Now Ms. Warner, do you have a few minutes to talk? It's very important. I'm sure Tedi wouldn't mind coming back later."

The jig was up. I was caught. I wouldn't be getting any more information from Angela Warner, at least not right now. Hopefully the sheriff – an actual professional – would have more luck.

"Of course, I can come back. In fact, I'll make a list of what I'm looking for and email it to you."

Angela hopped up from her chair, not happy about losing a possible commission. "I'm sure this won't take but a few minutes. We could drive out to the new housing development near the highway and look at some of the models."

I wouldn't live there for free. Every house looked exactly the same. How incredibly boring. What did it say about the residents there that they lived in beige cookie cutter houses? The only way they knew which one was theirs was by the house number on the mailbox.

Garrett pulled himself up to his full height and noisily cleared his throat. "That's where I live."

Of course, it was. Another big reason not to move there.

I made a show of checking my phone, scrolling through

messages. I'd received one from Missy while I'd been here. "Wow, there's a small emergency at the inn. I need to fly. Angela, thank you so much. I'll send you that list and then perhaps we can meet again."

When Garrett isn't standing over my shoulder.

Angela had lied so smoothly but I know what I saw and obviously I wasn't crazy, because the sheriff was here, too. That meant she was a suspect, so it looked like I would be house hunting for the foreseeable future.

On to see Missy and find out just what was going on in her life. After thinking about her story, I wasn't so sure she was telling the truth, either. Moving away didn't sound like something Dylan would ever do and coming over in the middle of the night to tell me about wasn't her usual behavior.

So why was she at the inn in the wee hours of the morning? I had to find out the real story.

Chapter Seven

I WANTED TO speak with Missy but the cafe was on the way, and I stopped in to talk to Daisy about the altercation between Jerome and the other man. She might have overheard more than Missy had.

The Grateful Raven was one of the most popular places to eat in Ravenmist and always busy. It always smelled delicious too.

Open from six in the morning until ten at night, it served a variety of dishes from comfort food to gourmet. My favorite was the complete turkey dinner. Almost any day of the year a hungry patron could walk in and get Thanksgiving dinner with all the trimmings. The only days that Daisy closed were Christmas and New Year's. She stayed open on Thanksgiving and Easter to feed anyone who might be alone on that holiday and she did it for free.

Daisy was a fascinating woman with an even more interesting past. She'd followed The Grateful Dead around for years selling beaded necklaces and tie-dyed t-shirts out of her van alongside her sister Grace. About twenty years ago, Grace had married an investment banker and now lived in New York City on the Upper East Side. But Daisy still had the stories... and she loved to tell them if you had the time to listen.

The bell above the door tinkled happily when I entered the cafe, waving to Myrna, one of the waitresses. She'd been the head cheerleader when I was in high school and one of the meanest girls I'd ever known, constantly making fun of my glasses. Somewhere along the line, she'd decided that we were friends and I wasn't the type to tell her off. The past was the past.

The aroma of freshly baked bread and roasting turkey hit me and my stomach growled. I could have just packed away a full meal and I still would have wanted that turkey with cranberry sauce.

Daisy, always bustling around, came up to me with a menu in her hand and slightly out of breath.

"Table for one or is Missy meeting you?"

Did I mention that Daisy's hair was tie-dyed today to match her shirt? She was still selling those shirts and necklaces but now to tourists. The whole restaurant was done in a sort of hippie theme. It was like taking a trip back to Woodstock.

"Actually, I'm headed to Missy's now. I was just hoping to talk to you. Just for a moment?"

Her lips twisted, Daisy finally nodded. "But only for a minute. We're slammed here with the festival and now a dead body."

I followed Daisy back to her office and she shut the door

behind us. "I know why you're here."

I probably also forgot to mention that Daisy is the town psychic. She's pretty good, too. I'm told she knew I was moving back to Ravenmist months before I did. I only wished she could have warned me about my ex.

"Sheriff Garrett suspects Missy."

Daisy scoffed and rolled her eyes. "She didn't do it but he wouldn't know any better. He's not one of us. Yet. He will be when this is over. His story has only just begun. I can feel the energy in the town changing. It's more intense than I've felt it before."

"More intense? What do you mean?"

"Just what I said. The energy all around this town has strengthened. It feels…different. I can't explain it but I know there's been a change."

"Do you know why?"

Shaking her head, Daisy shrugged. "My gift doesn't work like that. I can only tell you what I see and feel. I can't tell you the reasons."

Fair enough. Who was I to question Daisy's gift? I didn't have one myself so I'd have to take her word for it.

"Did you see or hear the argument between Jerome Bergstrom and the other man?"

"Everyone did. They were loud and angry. I had to tell them to quiet down or take it outside."

"What did they do?"

"The recently deceased left but I heard him say to the other man that the discussion wasn't over. It sounded like a threat."

Then Jerome had ended up dead hours later. Hmmm.

"Did you hear what they were arguing about?"

Leaning a hip against her desk, Daisy nodded. "Not every single word because I was busy and you know how loud it gets in here, especially during the lunch rush. But I did hear the words 'theft' and 'police.' I'm not sure which one of them is the thief but I did hear the deceased yell to the other man he couldn't do it. Whatever 'it' is. Mostly they just called each other names. Those everyone heard loud and clear. The other stuff they were more quiet about. I don't think they wanted that to be public knowledge."

The plot thickened… Was Jerome a thief or was the other man? Was Jerome's death some sort of karmic action? I was a firm believer in karma, although sometimes it was slow in coming and I wasn't around to watch it in all its glory.

"I don't suppose you caught the other man's name? Did he pay by credit card?"

"Sorry, he threw cash down on the table and stomped out right after the other one left. I don't remember hearing his name, either. I wish I could be more help."

"It's okay, but will you call me if you see the man again? Anytime, day or night. I'm not going to let the sheriff continue to think that Missy did this. There are plenty of other suspects."

Lorna, Angela, and the mysterious man Jerome had argued with were high on my list.

"You don't think the sheriff can solve this case? He's supposed to have all that experience from Chicago."

"I'm sure that he can," I said, not wanting anyone to think that I didn't have confidence in Garrett. "I just want to give him a hand. Since he's looking at Missy suspiciously."

Daisy's expression told me that she didn't quite buy my story but technically it was the truth. The fact that I wasn't sure that Jackson Garrett was able to look at this situation with fairness wasn't anything that I wanted blasted around town. It would get back to him and he already made my life difficult as it was.

"I'm sure the murderer will be in custody soon."

I thanked Daisy again and turned to head out but paused, wanting the answer to one more question.

"Daisy, have you ever seen a ghost here in Ravenmist?"

The older woman's lips turned up at the corners. "Having doubts?"

"No, there are so many stories but I've never seen one."

"Yet," Daisy replied firmly. "You haven't seen one *yet*. But you will. And yes, I have seen a ghost. It was when I was a child. My grandmother passed on but she came back to tell me that everything was okay and that she would watch over me. I felt real at peace after that. Haven't seen one since but I know they exist. I can feel their energy all around me. I just can't see them."

Thanking Daisy again, I headed out of the cafe and down the street toward Missy's place. There were so many unanswered questions but I knew one thing for sure. My best friend was no killer. But she had told a lie to the sheriff. I'd been thinking about it and it really didn't make much sense.

What was she hiding?

Chapter Eight

MY NEXT STOP was Missy's bookstore on Howling Creek Road, just around the corner from the inn. I was following my gut and it was telling me that her story about Dylan didn't make any sense. Not that I was going to let the sheriff know that.

When I got there, she was unboxing new books and placing them on the shelves, her back to the front window. The store was closed today but she ushered me in when I knocked on the door.

"Is the inn still crazy with people?" Missy asked me as she poured me a cup of coffee. Shrugging off my jacket, I wrapped my hands around the steaming mug of caffeinated goodness and took a sip. There was a definite chill in the air today despite the bright sunshine.

I settled onto one of her comfortable old couches near the crackling fireplace in the corner of the old building. Tucking my feet under me, I was content for the first time that day. "It is and can I say I'm glad to be here. I thought once the food ran out that everyone would leave but I underestimated the allure of a local murder."

"We haven't had one that I can remember. I think my parents said the last was about thirty years ago, so we would have been too young to know what was going on."

"The sheriff is getting on my nerves."

That made Missy laugh out loud. "He's always getting on your nerves, but there's definitely some chemistry between you two when you're in the same room."

"If you mean I want to smack him on the head with a beaker or a Bunsen burner, then yes, we have chemistry. And I'm not a violent person."

"He'll figure out our ways. He's still new."

"That's what Daisy said."

"She's a wise woman. She told me you were coming back to town."

"She also said that dinosaurs were making a comeback."

"Maybe she meant in the movies."

"I don't think that's what she meant. All I know is if dinosaurs do make a comeback, I'm totally getting one. A nice herbivore. I can keep him or her out in the back of the inn. Lots of space and leaves."

"Dinosaurs can't live in cold weather. If they do make a comeback it won't be here in the middle of the cold plains of Illinois."

"There's always a catch."

Missy sat down on her favorite red velvet chair and stretched out her legs toward the fireplace, wriggling her sock-clad toes.

"Getting back to the sheriff...when you came back from Chicago you were a little strange, too. You talked too fast and you were always in a hurry."

"I don't think my fast talking was from the city so much as being married to a man who had the attention span of a two-year-old. If I didn't talk fast he wouldn't listen."

"You're well rid of him."

Truer words were never spoken. I'd shed a hundred and seventy-five pounds of annoying male and my life was better for it.

"I can't believe you're defending the sheriff. He thinks you're a suspect."

"To be fair, he hasn't ruled out anyone as a suspect. Even you."

"Aren't you upset?"

Shaking her head, Missy stretched her feet closer to the fire. "No. I didn't do anything wrong so I'm not worried."

"Of course, you didn't." This seemed like a good opening in the conversation. "So what's this about Dylan getting a new job and wanting to move? I was shocked when you said that."

"Dylan always has a lot of irons in the fire."

No, he didn't. He was content small-town guy who was so laid back he was almost comatose.

"What kind of job was he offered? When does he have to move?"

Missy avoided my gaze and shifted in her chair. "He won't move if I don't."

"You didn't say what job it was. What company wanted to hire him?"

My best friend since we were five was lying to me and I didn't know why. In no way did I think she'd killed Jerome Bergstrom but something fishy was going on.

"Does it matter? He's not going to take it."

"Then why were you upset?" I pressed, determined to find out what Missy was hiding. As far as I knew she and I hadn't had a secret from each other since junior high when she'd kissed Arnold Farnsworth behind the hay bales at the fall festival. It wasn't a secret for long.

"Because I didn't know he wasn't going to leave until today."

She still hadn't looked at me. She was lying through her teeth. Time I called her on it.

"Why are you lying to me? This isn't like you. I know you're not a killer but your nose should be a foot long by now. I thought I was your best friend."

"You are my best friend."

Missy's voice sounded sad and I didn't know why. Why would she be sad that we were friends?

"You don't sound happy about it."

Finally looking at me, her eyes were bright with tears. "I've been keeping a secret from you."

A bar of fear took up residence in my chest. From the look on Missy's face, whatever she had to tell me wasn't going to be pleasant. This was more than stealing a kiss behind a hay bale.

"This is becoming a trend," I murmured. "First my parents

and now you. I hope you have better news than they did. You aren't sick, are you?"

Her brows pulled down and she shook her head. "I'm not sick. But what about your parents?"

Relief flooded my body and I sagged against the shabby cushions with a sigh. "Thank god. I don't think my heart can take much more of this. I came back home to avoid stress."

"Are your parents sick?"

There was panic in Missy's tone and I needed to put a stop to it. This was how stories started in this little town.

"No, they're separated. They say they're getting a divorce."

I didn't realize how upset I was by their news until I heard the acid in my own voice. I was angry at my parents and their complete disregard for our family.

"A divorce?" Missy sucked in a breath. "After all of these years?"

I threw up my hands. "Exactly. That's what I said. You're old. What's the point?"

Her lips twisted and she was trying not to laugh. "I don't think calling them old was the best idea. How did they react?"

"Not well. Oh, and this is the best part – my sisters all knew months ago. They didn't want to tell me because it might bring up bad memories and make me emotional. Isn't that a crock?"

"You are emotional."

"Whose side are you on?"

"Is it a war? Seriously, they must be very unhappy to take such a drastic step."

I had thought about that. I didn't want my parents to be miserable but they hadn't seemed upset today.

"You should have seen them standing in my kitchen telling me the news. It was like they were announcing the destination of their yearly vacation. They didn't seem upset at all. Apparently, they're still friends. Buddies. Pals. Is that even normal? I'm not having outings with my ex and trading recipes." I shook my finger at Missy. "And now you're lying and keeping secrets from me. What is happening in my life?"

"I have a good explanation as to why I was at the inn last night."

Here we go. Finally, the real story.

"It wasn't what you told Garrett is it?"

"No, he wouldn't have believed the truth."

Cynical jerk.

"Will I believe it?"

"I'm not sure but I hate keeping this from you. I don't like us having big secrets like this from one another. I just can't keep quiet anymore."

So it was a big secret? Wracking my brain, I couldn't think of one thing that Missy might be keeping from me. We both appeared to be living our lives completely out in the open. Had something happened when I was in Chicago, perhaps? A secret lover? That would be romantic but so unlike my best friend.

"So tell me."

"You have to promise to keep an open mind."

My mind was so open it was practically falling out of my

head and into my lap.

"I promise."

"And not jump to any conclusions. You have to hear me out."

I was beginning to think that my family and friends didn't have a great opinion of me.

"I will."

"Promise?"

I crossed my heart just as Missy had done with the sheriff. It was good enough for us when we were five and it was good enough now.

"Promise. Now spill it."

Sitting up straight in her chair, Missy took a deep breath. "I'm going to tell you the truth now."

So get to it.

"I'm ready for it."

"I was at the inn to collect Jerome Bergstrom's soul after he died. I'm the Grim Reaper."

Okay, maybe I wasn't as ready as I thought.

A murder, a divorce, and now my best friend thought she was the Grim Reaper. My life in Chicago wasn't looking too bad in comparison.

Chapter Nine

I WATCHED DUMBFOUNDED as Missy transformed back and forth from her usual self in worn blue jeans and a sweater to a foreboding figure in a dark cloak carrying a scythe. Foreboding but short. Being a reaper hadn't given her any extra height.

"So you can just change at will? Anytime? That could have been your Halloween costume every single year."

A lame attempt at a joke because I was still blinking my eyes every time she transformed. Missy would go a little blurry, the air around her went cooler, and then snap…she looked different.

It appeared that making a joke about walking death was in bad taste because Missy was giving me a sour look. Who knew death wasn't hilarious?

"This is business, Tedi. This isn't a joke."

It kind of was. The only way I could deal with this was to find it funny. Otherwise, I might have to start drinking. Heavily. In fact, I hadn't ruled it out.

"A business? Do you have a performance review and health insurance, too?"

"I do, although the benefits kind of suck," she sighed, sitting back down and draping her jean clad legs over the arm of the chair. "The pay isn't great either but it's a family business. Ethan is the oldest male so he was supposed to do it, but he went into the military and I got the job by default. It's not so bad. If I move enough souls a quarter I can earn a bonus."

"Wait...what? A bonus? Move souls? A family business? How can being a Grim Reaper be a family business?"

Grimacing, Missy took a gulp of her own coffee. "Technically, I'm a Reaper. The actual Grim Reaper can't be everywhere in the world. He's not Santa Claus, you know. So he or she has associates like me. I take care of this county and the three others surrounding it."

It made perfect sense, except that none of this made any sense. She was a reaper but she wasn't Grim. And wait...was Santa Claus real, too?

"And just where is the Grim Reaper located? New York City? London? Rome?"

"Sarasota, Florida," Missy said calmly. "You've met him. He's my Uncle Ralph. You know, the one that likes to play got your nose with the babies. He's just one in a long line from my family over the centuries."

Missy's Uncle Ralph was a loud, overweight man with a distinguished hairline who had owned a string of sandwich shops on the East Coast for years before he retired. Whenever he'd come to visit he'd bring me one of those huge rainbow lollipops that they only sold in candy stores.

I had accepted candy from the Grim Reaper. I wasn't sure

how to feel about that except that I wasn't going to do it again.

"Sarasota," I repeated slowly, trying to picture Uncle Ralph in dark robes carrying anything but that lollipop or the Bud Light he preferred as a beverage. "This is hard to wrap my mind around. So what exactly do you do? And better yet, what did you do for Jerome?"

"I shepherd souls to their final destination. That's what I did for Jerome, although I have to say he didn't go easily. He argued the entire time. I had to convince him he was really dead. That's common, actually. People don't like to hear that they're dead and I'm usually the one breaking that news."

That sounded like Jerome. I was beginning to believe that my best friend was the Grim Reaper.

It had been one long day and it wasn't over yet.

"Can you be more specific about this final destination? And how you get your bonus?"

Rubbing her chin, Missy didn't answer for a long moment. "Okay, so here's the deal. I'm supposed to inform people of their death and then lead their soul to their final destination."

"Which is?" I pressed. "You take them to the pearly gates?"

Chuckling, she smiled at my question. "I take them to the light. I don't know which way they're going to go until their soul actually moves on."

"I would imagine those that know they're going…downstairs…aren't too anxious to go."

Her smile fell and her lips tightened. "Some souls don't want to move on either because they don't believe they're dead or they just don't want to go. They're pig-headed and stubborn."

Apparently, this was a sore subject for my friend.

"You can't make them go?"

She shook her head. "I can try and convince them but ulti-mately the decision is up to them."

"And if they decide not to?"

"Then they stay here in this realm in a sort of purgatory state. A ghost, if you will."

My breath caught and my heart skipped a beat. "So there really are ghosts? They're real."

I knew it. I knew it. I knew it.

"Of course, they're real. This town has tons of ghosts. I should know because every soul that I can't convince to move on is a black mark on my annual review. I get dinged on my bonus, too. We have souls still in this town from when my great-great-great-grandfather was the Reaper. Maybe even before."

"I've never seen a ghost, though. How is this possible?"

"Ghosts don't like to be seen, I guess. I usually only see them when I'm in my robes. The rest of the time I'm as human as you are."

"Can you take me on your next soul collection? I want to see a ghost."

Missy was already shaking her no before I finished my query. "That's not how this works. I only got to go along when my mom couldn't get a babysitter. Besides, do you really want to see dead people? It's usually not a pretty sight. Jerome Bergstrom sure wasn't."

About Jerome… If Missy was there…?

"So you saw him die? You saw who killed him? Why didn't you just tell Garrett?"

"I get a text after they die so by the time I get there any self-respecting killer would be long gone. I didn't see anyone, but even if I did, how could I possibly explain that to the sheriff?"

Jackson Garrett wasn't the type to believe in ghosts or Grim Reapers. He'd been more than clear about that when his son had wanted to see a spirit.

Hah! Take that, Sheriff. I was right. There are ghosts in Ravenmist. And a Reaper. She was my best friend. Instead of disbelief I actually felt a sort of pride. Missy had an important job and it sounded like she was pretty good at it.

And here I was…really okay with the whole story and not fainting or screaming. Delirium was awesome.

"I can't believe you've been keeping this secret from me since we were kids."

"I didn't want to. I really wanted to tell you when you came back to town and were voted the head of the paranormal society. That meant you were open to this."

I was open to it, although I wasn't entirely convinced I wouldn't wake up soon and the entire day would have been a bad dream. Nothing that had happened would have seemed likely the day before, especially my friend being the Grim Reaper. That was truly out of left field.

Another thought occurred to me. "We still have the problem of you being a suspect. I don't suppose Reapers have any cool

Jedi mind tricks? Can you make the sheriff think you're innocent?"

Giggling, Missy shook her head. "Sorry, we don't have any party tricks like that. We can erase a few seconds of a person's memory so that if they accidentally see us they forget."

"You should have done that to the paper boy."

"I would have but I didn't know. It's too late now."

"So what do we do?"

"It will all work out. They don't have any proof because I didn't do anything wrong. It will all blow over and the sheriff will find the real killer."

Missy might trust that justice would win out but I wasn't so sure.

Lorna regretted marrying him, Angela kissed him, and what about that man that Jerome was arguing with in the cafe? And the most important question...

"So tell me about Santa Claus. Is he real, too?"

Chapter Ten

I COULDN'T STAY at Missy's bookstore forever, although it was far more peaceful there than the inn. I had to leave eventually and I half-heartedly walked back to my home hoping that the citizens of Ravenmist would have seen fit to go back to their own places of residence.

When I opened the front doors I was thrilled to see that most of them had done just that. Not feeding their empty stomachs appeared to have worked wonders. There were only a few stragglers now and they were mostly inhabiting the bar area that had opened only an hour before. To my surprise Lorna was sitting at a table with an unfamiliar man. They appeared to be deep in conversation, barely noticing anyone else.

Curious, I approached the bartender who was pouring tequila shots and placing them on a tray along with salt and limes. I didn't know exactly which patrons had ordered all of these shots but I had a decent idea that it was the rowdy locals tucked into the large corner table across the room. Hopefully, none of them had driven to the inn.

"Hey Neil, how's it going tonight?"

Neil was a big, burly man but incredibly soft-spoken. He could be quiet and mousy until a patron got out of line. Then heaven help them because Neil could go from zero to hero in about five seconds flat.

He handed the tray off to the waitress before answering me. Yep, it was headed to the loud table.

"Pretty good. I think most of these people are still hanging around hoping to see something exciting."

They were living in the wrong town.

"All they're going to see is their lunch coming up backward at the rate they're going. Don't hesitate to cut them off and if they give you any guff about it call me." He wouldn't need to. Neil could easily handle anyone. Casting a glance toward Lorna and her friend, I could see the man's face more clearly now. He definitely wasn't anyone that I knew or was staying here at the inn. "How long has Mrs. Bergstrom been here?"

If Neil thought it strange for me to ask, he didn't say anything. "About half an hour. They're on their second round. He's drinking an import on draft and she's having white wine."

At least they weren't doing shots, too. My stomach gurgled, letting me know I hadn't eaten since lunch. I'd grab a snack and keep an eye on these two from the kitchen.

"If you need me, I'll be in the kitchen grabbing a bite."

Lorna waved to me as I turned from the bar. "Tedi! Tedi, I need to speak with you."

Stopping at their table, I gave her my best professional smile. "Mrs. Bergstrom, how can I help you?"

"First, just call me Lorna. After all we've been through here I think you can call me by my first name."

Okay, we were going to be chummy. Interesting.

I took a side glance at her companion but he hadn't spoken yet. He was handsome though, blond and tan. Sort of a California surfer look in a double breasted blue suit. An expensive one, if I wasn't mistaken. I'd known lots of men like him when I'd lived in the city. My ex had been one of them.

"Thank you, Lorna. How can I help you?"

"I haven't introduced you to my attorney, Adam Taylor. Adam, this is Tedi Hamilton. She owns this inn." I shook his hand while his gaze traveled from toes to my nose. Was he sizing me up? I could do that, too.

"It's nice to meet you, Mr. Taylor."

"It's very nice to meet you, Ms. Hamilton. Please call me Adam, and may I call you Tedi? That's such an unusual name."

"It's short for Theodosia," I replied, extricating my hand from his. He'd held it a little too long. "Welcome to Ravenmist."

"Adam is a…family friend…and he's here to support me. I don't suppose you have a room you can put him in? The sheriff won't let us leave but he didn't say I couldn't bring people here."

I was completely booked up for the festival but I had a gut feeling that not everyone had heeded Garrett's warning and stayed put. Worst case scenario I could probably get him a room a few towns over.

"Let me check. Will you be here in the bar for a few minutes?"

They both said they would so I headed straight for the front desk. The inn might be old but I had installed some nifty computer software to help manage the guest rooms and the books. A few keystrokes told me that not everyone had done exactly what Garrett had told them to do.

He was going to be furious but what had he truly expected? That everyone was just going to sit around and wait?

"I've been looking for you all day. Where have you been?"

Sighing heavily, I looked up from the screen to see Sheriff Garrett leaning over the front desk and wearing a scowl. As usual.

"It's so nice to see you too, Sheriff," I said sarcastically. "Did you miss me? How sweet."

"I need to talk to you."

What a charmer. He was a real *people* person.

"So talk."

He gestured toward the bar area. "Who is that man with Lorna Bergstrom? I've never seen him before."

"That's because he's not from here. Adam Taylor, her attorney. He's looking for a hotel room so he'll be staying for awhile."

The smile that bloomed on Jackson Garrett's face was one of pure smug satisfaction.

"She's lawyered up. That means she's scared."

"You think she did it then?"

Hopefully, that meant he was done suspecting Missy.

Leaning a hip against the counter, he stole one of the mints from the candy bowl. "The spouse is always a suspect until they're cleared. She hasn't been cleared as far as I'm concerned. No one has."

"Not one person?" I asked, exasperated with this investiga tion. "What have you been doing all day?"

"Just watching soap operas and eating bonbons. Seriously, a murder investigation takes time. I suppose you think you could do better?"

"I couldn't do worse," I grumbled. "You can't keep a bunch of people hostage in town while you wander around hoping the murderer jumps out of a bush and confesses. Do you even have a plan?"

I'd hit a nerve because Garrett's face had turned an unbecoming shade of red. He wasn't so handsome now. As for chemistry? Not so much.

"Of course, I have a plan, woman. Just because you don't know enough about police work to see it doesn't mean it's not there."

Thank goodness, then.

"Then you'd better get to it and fast, Sheriff, because tomorrow is Sunday and most of these people will be up before dawn and on the road back to wherever they came from. Some have already flown your chicken coop."

That news did not go over well. He slapped his hand on the counter and leaned far across it so he and I were almost nose to nose.

"What do you mean?"

Clearing my throat, I took a step back to install some personal space between us. He'd been far too close. "I mean that I now have empty rooms. You said yourself that you couldn't make people stay."

"You didn't stop them?"

There was frustration in his tone but I wasn't going to let him foist this off on me.

"Was it my responsibility to do so? You've had deputies milling about this place all day sucking up free food and beverages from my kitchen. Don't you think one of them noticed a few people walking out with luggage and getting into their car? If they didn't stop them I'm not sure why you think I should."

"Because they couldn't stop them," he muttered under his breath. "I am not happy."

"That makes two of us, Sheriff. But I do have some good news if you want to hear it."

Scraping his fingers through his hair, he gave a sad sigh. He probably was exhausted and tired. Hungry, too. I should probably offer to feed him.

If he promised to leave Missy alone, I'd fix him a five-course meal personally.

"I would love to hear something good right now."

"None of the people that checked out were strong suspects. The Millers didn't even know the Bergstroms and were in bed early because of Mrs. Miller's allergies. The Shuberts are about eighty if they're a day, so I doubt they could hold down a grown man and drown him. And last but not least are the Sinclairs.

They only live one town over, so if you want to talk to them it's only a fifteen-minute drive, depending on traffic. They come here every year and are completely delightful. I don't think they're your killers."

"How do you know who are suspects?" he growled but the red in his cheeks had subsided. He was calmer than he'd been only moments before.

"I would imagine the family, friends, and business associates. Missy said that Jerome had an argument with another man at the Grateful Raven yesterday. Have you found him yet?"

"No."

"He might be staying in a hotel in another town. Have you checked?"

"Tedi, I'm not discussing my investigation with you."

"I'm just trying to help."

"Then stop. I don't need any help."

"Everyone could use help, Sheriff."

"For the love of God, I don't need help. This isn't my first murder."

"It's the first murder for many in this town, so excuse us if we're a little shaken. I found him and that's a sight I'll see in my nightmares."

Garrett's expression actually softened and he almost looked nice. "I wish you hadn't seen that."

"You and me both. Now I'm headed into the kitchen to get some food. When was the last time you ate?"

The air seemed to leak out of him and he slumped against

the counter. "I had half a sandwich in the car about one o'clock."

That was worse than I'd thought. He might not be my favorite person but I couldn't let him starve. He and his son were basically bachelors and who knows if they even had any food in that house.

"You'd better come into the kitchen and fix yourself a plate then. You can take a to go box to Tyler, too."

Garrett opened his mouth to say something – maybe to tell me where I could put my hot meal – but then seemed to think better of it. "Thank you. I appreciate that."

He'd learn eventually. We'd put the small town into him whether he liked it or not.

Chapter Eleven

THE SHERIFF WAS at my front door first thing in the morning vetting those that were checking out to make sure that he had their names, phone number, and addresses. Technically, I had all of that information but I'd told him over dinner that I wasn't all that comfortable giving it to him. It felt like a breach of trust between me and my guests. To my surprise, he wholeheartedly agreed and said that he'd deal with it. I hadn't really known what that meant until he was standing in my lobby at o-dark-early in the morning before I'd even had a cup of coffee.

"There's that guy again. I need to meet him."

Garrett was eyeing Adam Taylor, who was currently sitting with Lorna, Roger, and Cherie eating breakfast.

"Why? He wasn't even here when the murder occurred. You should be talking to Angela or Lorna. Even Roger and Cherie. They might have had motive, too. And that guy at Daisy's."

Another sigh. He was doing that quite a bit around me. Apparently, I frustrated the heck out of him.

"He's friends with the Bergstroms and the Mullaneys, correct?"

"Yes."

"Then he might know something that they aren't talking about. He might let it slip."

"He's an attorney. I doubt that."

Garrett's smiled widened. "That's the difference between you and me. While you were fast asleep with visions of ghosts in your head, I was checking out Adam Taylor. He's a real estate lawyer. Not a criminal one. If that's who Lorna's getting her advice from I've won the lottery."

"He still went to law school."

"He did indeed. Now I have a favor to ask you."

"A favor?" I echoed. Now this had all of my attention. Garrett Jackson was about to ask me for a favor.

"A favor," he confirmed. "Tyler has somehow gotten all caught up in the history of the town. He wrote a paper about it for school and now it's all I hear about. He wants to join your ghost hunting club and I want you to talk him out of it."

Now that I knew for sure that ghosts were real I couldn't stand the thought of discouraging anyone who had an interest in the paranormal. I may not have seen a ghost yet but there was real hope that I would. If my best friend was to be believed, and I'd seen the Reaper robes with my own eyes, Ravenmist was chock full of spirits that wouldn't cross over. Missy wasn't happy about it, either.

"Sorry, can't do it. And it's not a ghost hunting club, by the way. It's a paranormal investigation society. Ghost hunting sounds like we want to shoot them and mount their heads on our wall. We're simply trying to communicate with the spirits of the dead."

"And that's not strange at all," Garrett said sarcastically. "Do you even hear yourself?"

"I do, and once again I'll say that I won't discourage Tyler. If he has an interest he should be allowed to pursue it. It doesn't hurt anyone. If he was interested in playing baseball would you ask me to talk him out of that, too?"

"Baseball is perfectly normal."

"In this town so is looking for ghosts. In fact, we're going to Missy's bookstore again tonight. She's been hearing voices and footsteps." I grabbed a stack of messages and tucked them in my pocket. I'd deal with them in my office. One of them was from Missy and she'd be the first person I'd call. "Good luck talking a teenager out of anything. The more you tell him no, the more he's going to want to do it. If I were you, I'd tell him that you think it's all really cool so he'll decide that it can't be if you like it."

I knew I'd messed up when the sheriff grinned in delight, practically rubbing his hands together like a villain in a silent film. Oh my stars, what had I just done?

"That's a fantastic idea, Tedi. Not only will Tyler join, I'll join up, too. It won't be too much fun hanging out with his old man."

Jackson Garrett on a paranormal ghost expedition? He'd scare all the spirits away.

MISSY HAD TO deliver a few rare books to a customer in a small town nearby and had asked me to go along. Desperate to get away from Lorna, Adam, and the rest of the suspects, I immediately agreed. We'd have a nice lunch at a cool cafe and then I'd return, hopefully in a better mood than I was right now. The thought of spending the evening with the sheriff had done nothing positive for my attitude.

But first I needed to make a quick stop at my parents' house. Mom had sent me a text asking for my copy of the house key. I could only assume that she was changing the locks now that Dad was moving out. That seemed like overkill since no one in Ravenmist locked their doors often anyway. Besides, Dad was no serial killer or even a thief. The most he might do is pop by to borrow some spices for his famous chili.

To my complete and total shock, Angela Warner's car was parked outside and there was a brand new For Sale sign on the lawn. Clearly, Peggy and Dan had lost their minds. Again.

Determined to stay calm, I found my mother in the kitchen with Angela and a platter of chocolate chip cookies. The house smelled delicious, which I assumed was the point. I'd read about the real estate trick.

"Hi, Angela. Nice to see you again. Mom," I said sharply, nodding to Angela who was wearing her bright yellow real estate blazer. "Can I speak to you?"

"Nice to see you," Angela replied with a smile, oblivious to my turmoil. "I'm glad to see you too. I'm working on some leads for us to go see."

For a moment I'd forgotten that I was supposed to be looking for a new home but then I remembered to respond appropriately. "That's great news. I'm looking forward to it. Mom?"

Peggy was paging through a stack of papers and studiously ignoring me but I wasn't going to be ignored today.

"Mom?" I said again, a slight edge to my voice that even Angela picked up on this time, her smile dimming slightly. "I really need to speak with you."

My mother set the stack of papers on the kitchen counter with a huff. "Fine, let's go into the bedroom and talk."

I followed Peggy into the large master bedroom at the back of the house before digging into my pocket and holding up the metal key that my mother had requested.

"I guess I know why you want this now."

Plucking the key from my fingers, Peggy didn't have the grace to look even slightly embarrassed.

"I was going to tell you today. I didn't know Angela was going to have people looking at the house so soon."

Someone was already interested in the house? How? It wasn't like Ravenmist was a hopping, trendy destination. Jackson Garrett was pretty much the last person to move into town and before that it had been about six months or more.

"Someone is coming to look at the house? What are you going to do if they want to buy it, Mom?"

"Sell it, and I don't particularly like your tone, Theodosia."

My mother's Southern accent was quite pronounced this morning which meant she was annoyed with me. Good. I was annoyed with her so we were a matching set. Peggy loved things that matched. Have you checked out the drapes and the throw pillows?

"Why do you want to sell the house?"

I tried to keep the frustration out of my tone. Peggy wouldn't react well to it.

"Because it's too much for me alone. Too much space, too much maintenance. I was thinking about moving into one of those cute townhouses on the edge of town."

That's where Garrett lived. Cookie cutter central. My mother had officially gone crazy.

"You hate houses that all look the same."

Peggy laughed and waved her hand in the air as if I was simply being silly or talking nonsense.

"I think hate is a strong word. They're not my preference but condos certainly have their uses. This way I can free up my time to have fun."

Fun? My mother wanted to have fun? She was too old to be thinking about having fun. She could break a hip or something.

Okay, okay, my mother wasn't that old. But when had fun become her priority?

"When you and Dad get back together, you'll wish you hadn't sold this place."

Her smile dropped and she shook her head. "Honey, your

dad and I aren't getting back together."

Of course, they were. They just didn't know it yet.

"I get that you're going through some sort of…midlife crisis, Mom. But selling the house isn't the answer. We grew up here. We were a family here. All our memories are in this home. Christmas, Halloween, Thanksgiving. How can you turn your back on all of that?"

My voice had gone up at least an octave. I hadn't realized how upset I was at the prospect of all of my childhood memories being sold out from under me like old paperbacks at a garage sale. Those memories had to mean something to her, too. Parents were always going on and one about the good old days after all, especially my parents. They didn't trust anything made after the year 2000.

"I am not having a midlife crisis." Peggy's voice had risen as well. "As for memories, I am not the keeper of this family's memory bank. We have videos and photos for that. If you're so upset, why don't you buy the house?"

"I don't need a four-bedroom house."

"Neither do I."

I didn't make a habit of raising my voice to my parents or getting angry. Usually I didn't have to. She and Dad had been fairly even-headed when I was growing up so I didn't know what to make of this.

"What about Dad?"

"What about him?"

"Does he know you're selling the house? He might want to

buy out your share. He loves this house."

My father had put in countless hours of work on this home and he'd always been proud of it.

"Of course, he knows. He doesn't want it either. It's too big."

At this point, I truly didn't know what to say. It was as if my parents were simply chucking out our family's memories into the dustbin of history.

"I suppose my sisters already know that the house is on the market."

"I was planning on calling them tonight."

Aha. They were going to be upset. Or at least they should be.

"They're not going to be happy, Mom."

Peggy sighed and placed her hands on my shoulders. "It's not my job to make you happy anymore. That's your job. I understand that you're upset about this. I truly do. But your father and I both want a fresh start. I would think you of all people would understand that. Isn't that why you left Chicago?"

Darn it, she had me there. I had come home wanting a new start. Scratch that. I'd badly *needed* a new beginning.

"It's just a shock," I finally replied in a small voice. Guilt was quickly kicking in. I didn't want my mom – or my dad – to feel badly. They were already going through enough. I might think the idea of a divorce was insane but they didn't. One of us was in denial and it might be me. "I didn't expect this. All of this."

"I know, sweetheart. I am sorry that you're hurting and I would like nothing better than to take all of that away but I can't. Not this time."

There was sorrow in her tone so now I felt even worse. My mother was going through a huge change in her life and I was acting like a spoiled brat. She didn't need that.

"I just want you to be happy."

Because I really did. I also wanted my parents to stay married. I wasn't sure those two items could peacefully co-exist.

"I am happy," she said with a huge smile. "I'm not going to pretend that all of this isn't stressful. It is. But for the first time in a long time, I'm excited about the future."

I couldn't rain on my mother's parade. I wasn't that petty. At least, I didn't want to be.

"We should go shopping or something," I suggested. "Make it a girl's day out."

Her eyes lit up and she clapped her hands together. "How about a weekend in Chicago? We can stay in a fancy hotel. My treat. I know you don't mind the city in small doses."

I loved shopping in Chicago. I loved the food, too.

"Let's do that." I paused, remembering that I had a murder to solve first or Missy might go to jail. "Just as soon as this dead body stuff is behind us."

"Is Sheriff Garrett close to an arrest?"

Not at all. He didn't have a clue.

"I don't think so but I would be the last person he'd confide in."

"He's a handsome man, sweetheart. You could do worse."

"Why is everyone trying to fix us up into a couple?" I marveled. "We don't even like each other."

Peggy shrugged. "Hate is very close to love."

"I don't hate him. I'm indifferent. Besides, I don't want or need a man in my life. They're nothing but trouble."

"The right man isn't."

Pardon me but taking love and marriage advice from my soon to be divorced mother didn't seem like a good idea. To keep the peace, I took the high road.

"I'll take your word for it. Now I do need to get going. Missy and I are heading over to Travistown. She's delivering some books and we're going to have lunch."

"At the cafe on Maple? They make their own bread daily."

They did, along with an assortment of desserts. The really fattening kind. We were heading into winter so I could cover a pound or two with a nice thick sweater.

Peggy walked me outside to my car as another vehicle pulled up in front of the house. Apparently, my heart could take two shocks in one day because I didn't pass out when I saw Roger and Cherie get out of the car. What were they doing here?

"They're looking at the house," a cheerful Angela chirped from right behind me. She must have read my mind along with sneaking up behind me. Not cool. "They want to have a place in the country for weekends and holidays."

"And they chose Ravenmist?"

"Cherie is very interested in the haunted history of the town."

Many people were but they didn't buy four-bedroom Cape

Cod houses to indulge their fascination. It did occur to me, however, that neither were acting suspicious or guilty. If I'd killed a man in a little town that I was visiting, I sure as heck wouldn't buy a home there and set up housekeeping. I moved the couple several notches lower on the suspect list. Their behavior simply didn't fit with how I assumed a killer would act.

Or maybe they're doing it to throw everyone off? That would be ingenious. Diabolical, even. Somehow though, Roger and Cherie didn't have genius murderer written all over them. Still, it was an interesting development that they were shopping for homes.

Did the sheriff know?

Chapter Twelve

I SPILLED MY tale of woe to Missy over iced tea and grilled chicken sandwiches on the most amazing homemade wheat buns. She listened sympathetically, nodding in all of the right places but I could tell she had something to say when I was done. I wasn't going to come out of this unscathed.

"Give your parents a freaking break. You're acting like a child."

The wisdom of a best friend is a warm and loving thing. Sometimes.

"I am not acting like a child."

"You are," Missy shot back. "Are you listening to yourself? You don't want your parents to get a divorce. I totally get that. No one does. But they're not happy, Tedi. They don't want to be married to each other anymore. Can you honestly tell me that you want them to stay married and unhappy so that you feel better about life? You're all grown up and theoretically you're supposed to understand the complexity of relationships by now."

"I don't want them to be unhappy."

"Then back off and let them do this. You could be more

supportive. You don't want to wish you had later."

"Do you hear a lot of regrets from people?"

I would imagine the Grim Reaper had a few stories to tell.

"A few. They rarely regret the things they do, only the things they didn't do."

"So that's your advice?"

Missy dabbed her lips with a paper napkin. "It is. Grow up and be nice. It could be worse, you know. They could hate each other and be asking you and your sisters to take sides. That would be awful."

That would be terrible. I loved both of my parents and would never want to take a side against the other.

"You've made your point," I said with a sigh. "I'll do better, I promise. Don't you think I deserve a reward? Maybe cheesecake? Or a chocolate mousse?"

Missy's eyes had gone wide and her hand flew in front of her open mouth. "Oh my god, I can't believe it."

She could have just suggested I skip dessert. She didn't have to act all horrified. I wasn't that out of shape. Geez, Louise.

"Okay, okay. I won't have anything. Nice way to tell me that not only am I being a child, I also need to push myself away from the table."

"Not you," she hissed, leaning forward so only I could hear. "It's him. The man that was arguing with Jerome Bergstrom."

I immediately tensed and began to look over my shoulder but Missy grabbed my hand. "Don't look. He might notice we're staring."

"Then don't stare at him."

Missy was still looking. "I need to make sure that it's really him."

"Is it really him?"

I desperately wanted to turn around and see.

"It's really him. What do we do now?"

Good question. Garett was twenty miles away and even if I called him, by the time he arrived the man could be long gone.

"We have to find out who he is. Get his name."

Missy nodded in agreement. "Great idea. How do we do that?"

My friend sure had a lot of questions that I didn't have quick answers to.

"Can I turn around and look now?"

"Okay. Drop your fork or something to make it look casual. He's in the second booth from the back near the restrooms. All alone. Dark hair and blue jacket."

I'm pretty sure I'd seen that move in several screwball comedies. It didn't bode well for being undetected while sneaking a peek.

So of course, I dropped my fork on the floor and then exclaimed that I was so clumsy loud enough for the table next to us to hear. Bending down to retrieve it, I took a quick look at the man that we'd been wondering about and looking for.

He looked like any other guy.

Dark blue windbreaker, faded denim jeans, brown shoes. His sandy hair was clipped short and his face was clean shaven. He was just a regular, average man having a cup of coffee. No sign above his head declaring him a murderer, no menacing snarl, or evil eyes. In fact, he appeared rather harmless, his figure less than imposing.

I picked up the fork and placed it back on the table. "He doesn't look like a killer."

"They never do." I must have looked surprised because Missy rolled her eyes. "What? I watch the true crime channel. I know what I'm talking about."

"We need to get his name, or maybe we should follow him when he leaves."

"Don't look," Missy whispered. "But he's getting his bill now. He's digging a credit card out of his wallet. I'm going to see what the name is on it."

I didn't even have time to respond before Missy was out of her chair and striding toward the man. My heart was in my throat and I wanted to call out to her to stop and come back, but I had to let her do whatever it is she was planning to do. Was she simply going to walk up to him and ask him his name? I wasn't sure I could watch it all unfold in front of me but I couldn't look away either.

It was like an accident on the side of the road. You don't want to slow down and look but you can't stop yourself from doing it.

Then right before she got to the man's table Missy tripped over her own feet, landing in a heap on the floor. The man jumped up from his seat to offer a hand and before I knew it,

Missy was standing right next to his booth.

My best friend was a genius. Those reaper genes were amazing.

The credit card was sitting on the table and she only had to take a quick look down to see his name. They spoke for a brief moment, Missy smiling and appearing to thank her rescuer. She headed back into the ladies' room and the man sat down at the table again. I had to sit there and wait until she came back, which was probably only a few minutes but it felt like an hour. In the meantime, the man paid his bill and left. I had to quell the urge to go after him, depending on Missy to have the information we needed. By the time she returned, I was a sweaty nervous mess.

"Tell me you got his name," I said before she had a chance to sit down. "Because I let him walk out of here without following him. I saw him turn right outside the door so I suppose we could catch up if we hurry."

"No need," Missy replied with a smug smile on her face. "I got his name and there was company name on the card as well. He's William Wagner and the company was Crown Financial Consulting."

"William Wagner," I repeated, turning that name over and over in my brain trying to find where I might have heard it before but nothing came up. It didn't sound familiar at all. "Never heard of him. But we need to let the sheriff know that he's here in Travistown. He's going to want to talk to Mr. Wagner as soon as possible."

Missy's brows shot up. "You're anxious to see Jackson Garrett."

"Not really, but he needs to know." I signaled the waitress. "Let's get our desserts to go. The sooner the sheriff arrests the killer the sooner he'll stop suspecting you or the townsfolk."

Then everything could go back to the way it was before. Boring and predictable. Just the way I liked it.

GRATITUDE DIDN'T LOOK like I thought it would.

"Have you lost your mind?" Garrett asked after I told him the good news. The sheriff had been in his office interviewing Adam Taylor when I arrived at the station. The charming attorney had smiled at me but didn't stop to chat, simply waving when he saw me. He hastily exited the building, leaving me with an already agitated sheriff. I don't think his conversation with the lawyer had gone well.

"I have not lost my mind."

"Are you sure? Because this guy could be dangerous, Tedi. What were you thinking?"

Missy had gone back to the bookstore and I wasn't going to throw her under the bus by saying that she'd acted on impulse.

"We were thinking that we somehow needed to get his name. I thought you'd be happy and grateful."

"If something had happened to you–" Garrett broke off and rounded his desk, coming to an abrupt halt in front of me. "It was a foolhardy thing to do. You and Missy could have been seriously hurt."

"Then I'd be out of your hair, Sheriff."

"Somehow I doubt it. You'd find a way to haunt me."

"You don't believe in ghosts."

"For you I'll make an exception."

"Then you don't think Missy is a killer anymore?"

His inner struggle was stamped clearly on his features, but one side must have won because he sighed, rubbing the back of his neck as if I'd put a big pain there.

"No, I don't. There are others who have far more motive. I'm still not buying her story as to why she was at your place so early in the morning, though. It seems fishy."

That's because it wasn't the truth but we couldn't tell him the real story. Or maybe we could. I'd never seen a grown man faint before. It might be fun.

Hiding my right hand behind my back, I crossed my fingers. "It seems perfectly reasonable to me."

"You're not a cop."

"And this isn't Chicago. Now are you going to question William Wagner or not?"

"I am, but first I'll do a quick background check on him. I want to know as much as I can about him before talking to him." Garrett wagged his finger in warning. "Now stay away from this murder case. No more sleuthing or whatever it was you two were doing. We don't need another dead body or two in Ravenmist."

"It's almost like you care, Sheriff."

"Only because the town would blame me for your untimely demise."

"It would be so sad if you didn't get a chance to thank me for helping you."

Another long-suffering sigh from the man. "Thank you, Tedi. You did help, although I still think you and Missy should have just called me."

It was as good as I was going to get so I'd take it and run.

"You're welcome, Sheriff. See you tonight."

More quality time together. The paranormal investigation started right after dinner.

Chapter Thirteen

TYLER HELD UP one of the handheld recorders. "This is so cool. Will this really catch a ghost talking?"

I nodded and continued adjusting the monitors on the table we'd set up in the empty apartment above the bookstore. We'd placed cameras on the sales floor, in the office, and in the storeroom. "It will. When we get to that part of the investigation it's best to be still and ask questions as if they're living beings. Pause in between each question to give them time to answer."

Garrett tried to hide his eye roll but I caught it and gave him an elbow in the ribs when I stood to grab a cable. As solid as he was, I think I hurt my elbow more than his ribs. "We'll do the investigation in teams, taking turns. When it's not your turn, you'll stay up here watching the monitors and being as quiet as possible so that we don't hear you downstairs. It's not the ideal setup but we can deal with it tonight."

"We can't stay all night, son," Garrett warned Tyler. "You have school tomorrow."

"Nothing important."

"School is important."

I didn't think Garrett was going to win this argument.

"I'm writing a paper on this," Tyler said with all the self-importance a teenager could muster. "This is homework."

"What class is interested in ghost hunting?"

"History, of course."

"I do not understand modern education," Garrett muttered under his breath.

"We're going to split into teams," I said loudly, wanting everyone's attention. This was the fourth time we'd investigated the bookstore so it wasn't a big draw. Missy and I were there as usual, along with Tyler and Garrett as new members in training. Elliott Farraday was there with his brother Lloyd. Since their family was one of the founders of Ravenmist they were hoping to speak with a spirit from their ancestry. "Elliot and Lloyd, do you want to go first?"

The brothers were heads down over a stack of papers and shook their heads.

"You go ahead," Lloyd said. "I brought some old blueprints of the building and we're going to study those first."

I'd done that during the first investigation but Lloyd and Elliott hadn't been there. I left them to their scholarly pursuits and turned to Tyler, who had long since abandoned trying to act cool. This fifteen-year-old wanted to hunt some ghosts. He reminded me of myself when I'd first started.

And now I knew ghosts were real and this wasn't a waste of time.

"Tyler, do you want to go with me?" I gave his father a withering look. "I guess you can go, too."

Garrett stood and grinned. "I think I will. What about Missy?"

Missy was fiddling with the monitors. "I'm going to stay and watch the camera feeds. You go ahead."

I led the two males down the stairs and paused at the bottom. "Let's keep the chitchat to a minimum. We'll walk through the three rooms and then find a place to sit down and just listen. We'll ask some questions and hope they'll talk to us tonight."

I'll give credit where it's due. Garrett kept his mouth shut for the most part and didn't make any sarcastic remarks the whole time. Even when it was our turn to watch the monitors he pitched in, asking lots of good questions. I could tell he'd done his homework about ghost hunting and the equipment we used. He might not believe in it but he wasn't being a jerk. When he was like this, I could understand why the town liked him so much.

Later that evening, Missy was watching the monitors with Tyler when she abruptly stood up, the legs of the chair scraping the concrete floor loudly. "Tedi, why don't you and I do a walkthrough?"

I hadn't paired with Missy all evening so that sounded good to me. She appeared anxious to get away from the monotony of the monitor bank. It wasn't the most exciting part of the job and she had been doing it for quite awhile.

"Sure, let's do it. Are you guys okay up here?"

Garrett, who had been talking to Lloyd and Elliott about the blueprints, took Missy's abandoned chair. "I can help Tyler. Take your time."

Missy took the lead this time, walking briskly down the stairs and into the well-organized storeroom. She was something of a neat freak and there was a place for everything back here. She had her spices alphabetized at home.

When I lingered she urged me toward the sales floor. "I saw something on the monitor."

Perking up, I followed her into the main area of the bookstore all the way to the back where she had a few overstuffed chairs so patrons could sit and read. Missy sat down on one and indicated that I should do the same. I lowered myself onto the soft cushions and let my gaze wander around the room. Just what had she seen?

"You saw something?"

She nodded, her gaze trained on a bookshelf against the wall. "Edward. He lives in this part of the bookstore. I rarely see him but he's been very active lately. Almost too active. I'm hoping he's ready to go into the light. It took him several years to even admit that he'd passed on."

I had to admit that I was intrigued, not just because this Edward was a real ghost but because he didn't want to go to the other side. Wherever that would be for him.

"Is he one of yours?"

"No, he was Grandma's. But that doesn't mean that I can't try to get him to cross over. He can't stay here forever."

"Why not? I like it here."

The voice came out of nowhere and I looked side to side and behind me but couldn't see a body to go with it. Missy shook her head in warning to me and placed her finger over her lips when I would have responded.

To my surprise, she slipped her foot under the cord from the camera to the outlet and surreptitiously tugged at it, hiding her movements with her body from the eagle eyes upstairs. The camera unplugged and I'm sure the monitor upstairs went dark. What would Garrett do?

"The sheriff will come down here to investigate the camera."

"Maybe. Maybe not. You told him only two people at a time down here and he's a newbie. Remember, he doesn't think there's anything to see so a camera malfunctioning isn't a big deal to him. There's a bunch of other cameras he and Tyler can watch. I'm hoping that he leaves it for a little while and just tells us about it when we go back."

"Aren't we supposed to be gathering evidence?"

"Yes, but Edward doesn't want the attention. Do you, Edward? Are you going to come out? I want to introduce you to my friend Tedi."

"Is she a reaper, too?"

"No, just the owner of the Ravenmist Inn."

Thank goodness I wasn't eating or drinking, because I almost choked on my spit when a full body apparition walked out of the bookcase and casually leaned against Missy's chair. Edward looked to be in his thirties perhaps, maybe younger, wearing a pinstriped suit. He had short dark hair and wire-rimmed glasses and he was pale. But then he hadn't seen the sun in a long while, I supposed. He was also slightly transparent but not as much as in the movies. If you weren't looking closely, he could have blended into a crowd of people. I wondered how many times I'd seen an actual ghost but missed it because they didn't look all that different from a regular live person.

"Edward, this is Tedi. Tedi, this is Edward."

Edward extended his hand so I did, too. I wasn't sure if I should touch a ghost or even if I could but he had no such qualms so I went with it. When he touched my skin, it felt slightly electric but not unpleasantly so. He leaned down and kissed my hand so gentlemanly I wondered how long he'd been gone. Missy had said he belonged to her grandmother and that, along with his clothes, had me guessing the 1950s.

"It's a pleasure to meet you, Edward."

"And you." He scowled at Missy. *"I'm not crossing over, so you're wasting your time."*

"I'm not here to nag you, although I should. Hasn't this nonsense gone on long enough? It's far past time."

"I know which way I'm going so you'll never convince me."

Oh. Had Edward been…evil in his life? He seemed to think his destination wasn't going to be pleasant.

"You don't know for sure."

"Trust me. I'm not going anywhere good, so I'm staying here. I like it. People coming and going. Lots of books to read. It's nice."

"I think you're making a mistake."

"You're only thinking about your quarterly bonus. I'm just a

number to you."

Missy hopped up from her chair. "That's not true. I really care about you. All of you. I just want you to be happy."

"I wouldn't be where I'm going," Edward said. *"So give it up. Now what brings you ladies here tonight?"*

"Another paranormal investigation," I answered, still not able to tear my gaze away from the spirit in front of me. This might be the single most amazing thing that had ever happened to me in my life. Or tied for it. The Grim Reaper being my best friend was right up there too. "The history of Ravenmist has many stories about spirits."

Edward grinned in delight. *"I remember them from when I was a kid. My dad told me those stories, and some of them were pretty scary. Then you get here and you realize that ghosts aren't all that terrifying. Only a few are."*

"A few?"

"If a person was a jerk in life they're probably not going to be a delight in death," Edward replied.

That made sense.

"What were you like?"

"A handful," Edward said crisply. *"Always getting into trouble. My poor parents went through hell. I think they were relieved when I died."*

"They weren't," Missy said sharply. "They mourned you for years."

"How did you…?" I didn't quite know how to phrase the question. Was it a social faux pas to ask a ghost how they got that way? "I mean…"

"*Car accident.*" Edward's smile faded. *"I don't want to talk about it."*

"That's fine," I replied hastily, not wanting him to disappear. I couldn't let this opportunity go. "None of my business, anyway. So I've done these investigations several times but I've never seen you before. In fact, I've never seen any ghost before and yet the town is supposed to be crawling with spirits."

Edward shrugged. *"I don't know. Most of the time we simply exist. We watch the world go by and enjoy the peace and quiet. It takes a great deal of energy to be seen by people and young ghost don't often have enough. When you're dead, time gets all fuzzy. It's not the same as when I was alive. I know decades have passed but it only feels like a few months or maybe a year. But something is going on. I've been feeling more restless and the other spirits have been feeling it, too. We can't rest easy the way we used to. We have a great deal more energy and we want to be active."*

"Why didn't you say something?" Missy asked, her mouth open in surprise. "I could send a message to my uncle and find out if something is going on."

"It's not our way to confide in reapers," Edward said, his tone tinged with disgust. *"You might use whatever's going on against us."*

"I would never do that," Missy protested, but it was clear the friendly bookstore ghost wasn't buying it. "I wouldn't. I swear."

"It doesn't matter because I don't know why we're all so restless. We just are. Maybe it's just time to wake up. We slept for awhile

and now we're awake and have more energy. Seems logical."

Since this statement came from a ghost I wasn't sure anything was really logical or made sense.

"I'm still going to ask my uncle," Missy mumbled, a frown on her face.

I had so many questions. "Can you leave the bookstore? Move around town?"

"If I wanted to I could, but I like it here. I've always liked to read." A book floated off one of the shelves and into Edward's hand. Wow. *"I'm especially enjoying this trilogy."*

I took a peek at the covers. This mid-century man who thought he was going someplace bad was reading the *Twilight* saga. Wait...

"Are vampires real, too?"

He looked at me like I was as dumb as a bag of hammers. He might be right. *"Of course not. That would be crazy."*

Said the ghost.

"Right. Of course. So if you can move around and leave the bookstore, I don't suppose you came to the festival this year?"

"I stopped by for a little while. I like the music."

"I don't suppose you know who committed the murder of Jerome Bergstrom?"

It was a longshot but I had to try. I had a brief happy image of solving the murder before Jackson Garrett.

"No, but you should ask Terrence."

"Who is Terrence?" I asked with trepidation. Was he...deceased as well?

Edward was looking at me like I was stupid again. It was starting to make me mad. I wasn't that dumb. *"He lives in your closet. He might have seen it."*

My closet. Since I was positive a real live human being didn't live in my closet that could only mean that I had a ghost in there.

And he'd seen me naked.

"Terrence is a ghost."

I didn't phrase it as a question.

"He's been in between since the 1920s," Edward said. *"He ran a speakeasy in town but was shot in a territory dispute by one of Al Capone's men. At least that's the story I heard. He might have died by choking, or from the flu, or food poisoning. It wasn't hard to pass away early back then."*

In between. An interesting turn of phrase for purgatory.

"And he doesn't pass over because…?"

"He's going the same way I am," Edward said, his arms crossed over his chest. *"He ain't going to go into the light and neither am I."*

Missy sighed. "You don't know for sure."

"Neither do you."

Edward had a point. Missy didn't know where they were going until they were on the other side. If they didn't want to go, did it hurt anyone that they stayed here?

"If Terrence exists, how come I've never seen or heard him?"

Although now that I was thinking about it, my room did have lots of unexplained noises. I'd always put it down to it being an old house. In addition, my stuff was always moving around. I'd place my brush on top of the dresser and I'd find it on the bathroom vanity. Was Terrence playing a game with me?

"He's quiet, doesn't say much. Plus, I already told you, we've been at rest for a long time. It's only recently that we've become more active."

The sound of footsteps on the stairs had three heads whipping around. Immediately Edward slipped back into the bookshelf before Garrett could see him, leaving Missy and I appearing to be alone.

Garrett pointed to the camera on the bookshelf. "I wanted to let you know that the camera is off. It's been off for a few minutes actually, but I didn't want to disturb you down here. Tyler said you might need to know right away."

"Thank you," I said, standing on shaky legs. My body and brain were beginning to catch up to the events that had unfolded here a few moments ago. I'd seen a real live ghost. Okay, maybe not a live ghost but a real one. I'd seen and talked to him. Heck, I'd touched him. It was a dream come true. "It's probably just a loose cable."

Missy bent down and picked up the cable. "And here it is. I've got it. Maybe we should break the investigation down for the evening anyway. I think everyone is pretty tired and we've got lots of recordings and footage to go through."

"That sounds like a great idea," I agreed enthusiastically. I didn't need to ghost hunt anymore. I'd found one. "I'll start pulling the cameras. Sheriff, you can take Tyler home and get him to bed if you like. We've got this."

"Absolutely not. If my son wants to hunt spirits then he has to do the grunt work, too. We'll get this done quicker with all of us helping."

The sooner we got out of here, the sooner I could go home and introduce myself to Terrence.

Ghost in residence at the Ravenmist Inn. I needed to talk to him badly.

Would he appear if I called to him?

Chapter Fourteen

I
T WAS FREEZING outside so in the spirit of teamwork and getting home where it was warm, everyone pitched in and helped break down the equipment. Tyler and Garrett helped us load Lloyd's van, all of us moving quickly in the brisk air. Lloyd and Elliott were our resident tech-geeks and they maintained all of our gear and it was their basement where it was all stored. Someday we were going to get an office or headquarters but today was not that day.

We'd placed the last monitor into the back when Garrett's phone went off, startling all of us but the sheriff. In his line of work, he was sure to be used to calls in the middle of the night but it had been so quiet as we'd worked that the ringtone was completely unexpected.

The brothers drove away as Garrett took the call, his expression sober. Ravenmist wasn't rife with crime so I couldn't imagine what had him so serious. Not another murder, surely? He hung up his phone and shoved it in his pocket, puffs of steam billowing from his mouth from the cold.

"That was a friend of mine who is still a cop in Chicago,"

Garrett said. "William Wagner is Jerome Bergstrom's business partner."

Business partner. Interesting. That put a whole new spin on the case.

"Then they must have been arguing about business that day."

Garrett shook his head. "We don't have any idea what they were arguing about. Conjecture is a dangerous thing, Tedi."

"Okay, they *probably* were arguing about business. How's that?"

"Better, but we really don't know. That's why I'll be talking to him tomorrow."

"Do you think he'll really tell you the truth?"

"I like to think I'd know if he was lying."

He would think that. There was no shortage of self-esteem there.

"Good luck then. Maybe he's the one."

"Maybe. Tyler, we need to get going. You have school to-morrow."

"I know, I know." Tyler gifted me with a huge smile. "Thanks for letting me join the group, Ms. Hamilton. This was awesome."

I only wished that he could have seen a real ghost. Perhaps next time.

"We're happy to have you. You did a great job tonight. And please call me Tedi."

"Thanks, Tedi! Goodnight."

The teenager grinned and sprinted off toward Garrett's vehicle, leaving me with the sheriff.

"He'll probably be up with the birds and no worse for wear," Garrett grimaced. "I'll be the one dragging all day. I used to be able to party all night."

I had vague memories of doing the same but these days I was happy to be tucked up by eleven at the latest.

"My mom always says that youth is wasted on the young. I'm beginning to think she might be right."

"Funny how parents get smarter the older we get." Garrett nodded toward my car. "I'll make sure you get going safely."

"This is Ravenmist, Sheriff. No one is hiding in my backseat."

Unless it was a ghost. If my closet had one, I suppose my car could, too.

"Did you even lock your car?"

I pulled up the handle without the keys. "Nope. No one does."

"I do."

"Then you get the safety award. Seriously, I'm all good here. Thank you. And I meant what I said, you and Tyler did great tonight. Your help loading up was especially appreciated considering the temperature out here."

My cheeks and lips were going numb, as a matter of fact.

"I'll just make sure your car starts."

The only reason I'd even driven to the bookstore was because of the cold. Normally I would have walked.

"That's very gallant of you. Thanks. I guess I'll see you to-morrow."

I didn't know why I'd see him tomorrow but his daily presence at my inn was becoming a habit.

The inside of the car wasn't much warmer than the outside and by the time the heat warmed up I'd be home. But I was out of the wind and that was something. Garrett was standing a few feet from my vehicle, his cold hands shoved in his pockets and his cheeks bright red. I waved as I backed out of the space, happy to be headed back to the inn.

My ghost hunt wasn't over. I wanted to talk to Terrence.

THE INN WAS quiet, all the guests asleep when I returned. The clerk at the desk tried to smile but ended up yawning. Night manager wasn't the most coveted of roles but it was important. Audrey did an excellent job working in the wee hours so she could go to school during the day. I didn't have any issues if she wanted to study on her shift as long as everyone was happy and taken care of.

Tiptoeing to my own apartment, I hung up my coat and kicked off my shoes. Already my home didn't feel the same since I now knew that I was sharing it with someone.

Assuming that Edward was even telling the truth. If he was the type that was worried about which way he was going in the afterlife, then I might not want to put too much stock into what he had to say.

After making myself a hot chocolate, I padded on stocking-feet into my bedroom. As usual, in my haste to get to the bookstore I'd left my closet door wide open. Pulling up a chair from beside the bed, I sat right outside that door, prepared to coax out an introverted spirit.

Was there such a thing as ghostly social anxiety?

"Um…hi. I'm Tedi, but you probably already knew that. I just talked to Edward at the bookstore tonight and he mentioned that you were here and that made me really want to meet you. He said your name is Terrence. Did I mention that I'm Tedi? Oh yeah, I did, didn't I? Well, it's short for Theodosia, which is a ridiculous name, don't you think? My mom is from the South and she named me Theodosia Elizabeth Virginia Evans Hamilton. Evans is her maiden name and Hamilton is our family name. I was married once but I never took his name, which was probably a good thing since we ended up divorced. He didn't care if I took his name. He said it was old-fashioned and I guess it is, although I hadn't given it much thought. What do you think? Anyway, I'd really like to meet you, Terrence. It would be great if you'd show yourself or at least talk to me."

That was quite the soliloquy and I needed to stop and catch my breath. How did one talk to a spirit? I'd spoken with Edward as if he was still alive, which is exactly what I'd told Tyler to do, but now that I was sitting here sipping hot chocolate and trying to convince a shy ghost to show himself I wasn't as sure as before.

"I get lonely sometimes and I thought you might, too. What do you do all day? Edward says he likes to read. I could get you some books if you want."

"I watch over the guests."

I heard the voice as clear as a bell but I didn't see anyone. Yet.

"They're interesting aren't they, Terrence?" I wanted to stand and look for the source of that voice but I forced myself to stay seated in the chair. If he was unsure about coming out I didn't want to scare him. That was a funny turnabout. A ghost afraid of a human. "I could do a reality show just about all the people that come and go here."

"I don't like your television."

I did watch too many baking shows. Clearly, Terrence found it boring. If I wasn't watching baking shows I was watching old black and white movies.

"It is sort of boring. What do you like to watch? I could turn the television on for you when I'm not here."

"Thank you, but there's no need. I watch the guests and listen to them," he repeated, the voice sounding closer this time.

My fingers tightened around my warm mug and I sat as still as possible, even as my heart sped up with excitement. Two ghosts in one night? Amazing. I'd waited so long for this and had thought it might never happen. I had two ghost friends. Not many could say that.

"Are any of them interesting?" I took a deep breath and plunged in. Patience had never been my strong suit. "Terrence, did you see who murdered Jerome Bergstrom?"

No answer this time. Had I upset or angered him?

"It's okay to tell me," I cajoled softly. "If you did or didn't see anything, it's all fine. But if you did, it would help us a great deal to find the killer. He or she needs to be brought to justice."

"Mr. Bergstrom wasn't a nice man. He was mean to his wife."

I hadn't known that. They hadn't seemed like the happiest couple in the universe but they hadn't been snarling at each other, either.

"Did he hurt her, Terrence? Physically?"

"No, but he wasn't nice to her. He ignored her and spoke mean to her."

"Did you see him being murdered?"

More silence, but then finally an answer.

"No."

I was actually kind of glad that he hadn't. That had to be an unpleasant sight even if you were already dead. Since he wasn't going to cross over he'd have to live with it for the rest of his–

Wait. He wasn't alive. He'd have to *deal* with it for the rest of his *in between*.

"Can you show yourself to me, Terrence? I'd really like to meet you. After all, you see me all the time."

I didn't want to think about how I'd looked on some of those occasions. Better to block that out.

More silence. I stayed quiet as well, letting him make the decision. I was sure that even if he didn't show himself tonight he would eventually.

"I don't think so."

"Okay," I said in my most soothing tone. "That's fine. Can we keep talking, though? How long have you been here, Terrence?"

His answer was immediate. *"Since 1925. My whole family was down with the flu and I died along with two of my sisters. There's a rumor around town that I worked for Al Capone but it isn't true. Not sure how it got started."*

His story was so incredibly sad. I wasn't quite sure what to say but it turns out I didn't have to. He wasn't done with his story.

"They've all gone over to the other side. But I'm afraid to."

"Why, Terrence?"

He probably missed his family terribly. Surely, he'd want to go with them?

"I stayed to keep a watch over my mom and my other brother. Make sure they were okay. I was the man of the house."

Terrence said it so proudly and my throat tightened with emotion. A question about the whereabouts of his father was on the tip of my tongue but I bit it deliberately, not wanting to bring out any more bad memories for the man.

Although he sounded young.

"You can cross over now, if you want to. My friend Missy can help you."

"I'm used to it now. I watch the lives of the guests. And you too, of course. I was particularly fond of your grandmother Rose. She would tell me the best stories about growing up on a farm. She

reminded me of my mom. You do too, a little."

Terrence had stayed because my grandmother Rose reminded him of his mother. Now my heart was aching along with the lump in my throat. In all the time I'd been ghost hunting I'd thought about the stories behind the people but this was far more. This was…personal.

"Thank you, Terrence. I can't tell you how much that means to me. You're a very nice young man and I'm glad that you're here."

Missy was going to kill me since I wasn't trying to persuade him to go into the light but he seemed perfectly content. After I got to know him I might ask if he wanted to rejoin his family.

"I didn't see the murder," Terrence said out of the blue. *"But I did see a woman that looked like his wife walking around outside that morning. Early. You weren't awake yet."*

Lorna? That certainly wasn't where she said she was. According to her, she was tucked up in her warm bed sleeping and she didn't have a clue that her husband had left their room. Another interesting turn. There were no shortage of suspects for Jerome's demise.

"Thank you, Terrence. I appreciate your help."

"You're welcome."

I wasn't ready yet to say goodnight to my new friend. I'd been tired earlier when I'd left the bookstore but now I was wide awake.

"Terrence, do you remember any of those stories my grandmother told you? I'm wondering if they're the same ones that she used to tell me."

"I remember them all. Do you want me to tell you one?"

More than anything. I'd loved Grandma Rose, too.

Chapter Fifteen

ANGELA ARRIVED BRIGHT and early at the inn. Wearing a huge smile and her gold real estate blazer, she waved at me from the front desk as I stumbled toward the kitchen for my first cup of the day. I wasn't sure I could take all that perkiness without massive amounts of caffeine, but it looked like I'd have to because she was making a beeline straight for me.

I'd stayed up far too late talking with Terrence and had thoroughly enjoyed our walk down memory lane. It was clear he held my grandmother in high esteem and anyone that loved her was alright in my book. I'd asked him if Grandma Rose had known of his existence and he'd confirmed that yes, she had, although quite late in her life. He'd never actually shown himself but they'd played silly games with each other. She'd place an object somewhere and he'd move it, hiding it so she'd have to look for it.

I'd asked him why he hadn't shown himself to her and he'd said that at the time he didn't have the energy to do so. It had only been recently that he'd been able to do it at will. That went along with what Edward had said. Ravenmist had received an injection of paranormal energy from…something, someone, or somewhere.

Now that I knew that ghosts were real I could turn my investigative energies to finding out why the spirits of our sleepy little town were suddenly waking up. But first we needed to find out who killed Jerome. I was sure it wasn't a ghost but a real live person.

"Tedi, I hope you don't mind me dropping by so early but I just had to tell you that I think I've found the perfect house for you. I was hoping you'd have time today to see it. I think it won't last long on the market."

Was there suddenly a real estate rush I wasn't aware of? I didn't have time to answer because Lorna had entered the lobby and she was pointing to Angela, her hand shaking with rage. Face bright red, she appeared to be trying to speak but couldn't quite get the words out.

"You," Lorna finally screeched, her lip curled in contempt and her finger wagging under Angela's nose. "You have some nerve showing your face here. You killed him. Someone call the police. This woman killed my husband."

That escalated quickly.

From the look of disgust on Angela's face if I didn't intervene right away we were going to have a cat fight on our hands. Right here in the lobby of the Ravenmist Inn. It definitely wasn't our first and it wouldn't be our last, but it just might be avoidable.

"Ladies," I said firmly, holding up my hands in sort of a

traffic cop stopping motion. "Let's not throw around accusations and names. Let's keep private business private."

I glanced over my shoulder to the dining room full of guests who would absolutely love a show to go with their meal this morning. Usually I just had a guy who played guitar on the weekends.

Lorna's lips pressed into a thin line. "She's the cheap harlot who was seeing my husband."

"And let's not call each other na–"

"You don't know what you're talking about," Angela said with a smug smile. "And the last thing I am is cheap."

Lorna was shaking her finger at Angela again. She was going to take an eye out with that thing.

"I know you killed Jerome," she hissed, her eyes narrowed and her cheeks scarlet. "I know you did it."

"Once again, let's not accuse–"

"Why would I kill Jerome?" Angela asked. "What possible motive did I have?"

Okay, that's a question that I wanted answered as well.

"Because he wasn't going to leave me for you," Lorna replied. "And you were angry about losing your meal ticket."

So Lorna had known about Jerome and Angela's affair? How long had it been going on?

"What makes you think he wasn't going to leave you?"

"He said so."

Angela smiled and shrugged carelessly. "He told me different."

"Then he was lying."

"To you, maybe. Jerry and I had a very open and honest relationship. He was leaving you and you were mad about that. It's not me that was losing my meal ticket. I can support myself just fine." Angela's cheeks went pink and she pointed to Lorna. "It was you that was going to lose out. You haven't done anything but shop and get manicures for years. You'd be the one losing your meal ticket. It seems to me that you have an even greater motive for killing your husband. Now that he's gone you have it all. The money, the house, the cars, the kids. Everything."

"You killed him," Lorna insisted, her voice rising again. She was beginning to attract the attention of the other guests. This wasn't a good idea but I had no idea how to stop it. It had taken on a life of its own. "You killed him because if you couldn't have him, then no one could."

"You're delusional," Angela declared. "I bet you killed Jerry. For the money and so you wouldn't have to go through a messy divorce."

"There wasn't going to be a divorce."

Her brow quirked, Angela slowly smiled. "Are you sure? Because Jerry knew about you and Roger."

I almost stumbled back and fell into a heap on the floor after hearing that news. Lorna and Roger? Was it true?

Lorna, too, appeared to be shocked by that news. Her once red face had gone pale and her hand had flown to her throat in a protective gesture.

"You don't know anything," she said, her voice choked and strangled. "It's not what you think."

I was thinking this all sounded sordid and icky. What were people doing in the suburbs, anyway? And did Cherie know? Was she anywhere around to hear this? With any luck she was still tucked up in bed.

"It's exactly what I think," Angela said confidently. "Jerry knew all about your Tuesday afternoon book club meetings and your Thursday workouts at the gym. He knew about it all. He just didn't care. He stopped loving you a long time ago. He loved me."

Both women fell silent, locked in a battle of wills. And a staring contest. The color had come back to Lorna's skin and she'd pulled herself up to her full height, a sneer on her lips.

"If he cheated on me, he would have cheated on you, honey. Do you truly believe he was going to leave me for you? Let me tell you, he wasn't. You're just one in a long line of women he's seen behind my back. You wouldn't have been the last. He likes them brunette and he likes them young. Even if he did leave me, he would have eventually left you too, when you got too old. Did he tell you that I'm wife number two?"

Sucking in a shocked breath, it was Angela's turn to go pale. "That's not true."

"It is," Lorna insisted. "I looked the other way and so did he. Our marriage worked because we didn't expect too much of one another. I didn't have any reason to kill my husband. But you did. He lied to you about everything."

I hadn't seen this altercation coming, nor the revelations. Perhaps I should have consulted with Daisy about it all.

"This is most interesting."

The sheriff's voice. When had he arrived? I'd been too busy to notice.

The two women felt silent, realizing that the sheriff may have heard far more than they'd wanted him to.

All this and before I'd even had a cup of coffee. It didn't bode well for the rest of the day. Plague and locusts couldn't be far behind.

"Sheriff," I said in greeting when no one else spoke. "To what do we owe the honor?"

"I was hoping to grab a coffee and a breakfast sandwich in your dining room on the way to the station. I'm supposed to be interviewing William Wagner this morning. Looks like I'll also be talking to these women as well."

"But–"

"Sheriff–"

Shaking his head, Garrett held up his hand, silencing them both. "You can both tell me your stories. At the station. And this time let's tell the truth, shall we?"

"I want my attorney," Lorna said, her voice shaky, whether with anger or fear I didn't know. Maybe both.

"You have that right," Garrett said. "You can follow me to the station. Just as soon as I get my breakfast."

"I don't need a lawyer," Angela sniffed disdainfully. "I didn't do anything wrong."

"That is also your right."

Garrett was looking at me, his brows raised expectantly. Right. Breakfast.

"I'll just run into the kitchen, Sheriff. Bacon or ham on that sandwich?"

"Whatever is easiest. I appreciate it, Tedi. Thank you."

At this rate, I was going to start liking the guy.

Fleeing into the kitchen, I asked the chef to quickly make up a sandwich for the sheriff while I poured two coffees. One for me and one for him. In the biggest cups we had. I had a feeling that we were both going to need all the coffee we could get.

William Wagner. Angela Warner. Lorna Bergstrom.

All suspects with motive. And Lorna had been seen on the grounds early in the morning by Terrence. Did I dare tell the sheriff? How would I even explain it?

A ghost saw your suspect right before the murder.

I'd hold off and see what came from his questioning. Maybe the murderer would confess.

And perhaps pigs might take to the skies of Ravenmist and sprinkle rainbow dust along Main Street.

Chapter Sixteen

AFTER SUCH AN eventful morning I was happy to retreat to my office with a second cup of coffee and a cinnamon Danish, plus a glass of water for the potted plant on my desk. A gift from my mother who had a bizarre sense of humor. Everyone knew I'd killed every single plant I'd ever owned, so she'd bought me a fern which she claimed was indestructible. I'd promptly named him Howard and begged Missy to help me keep him alive.

My mind was whirling with all that I'd learned this morning and I couldn't help but wonder what was going on in the sheriff's interrogation room. He had them lined up today, which he hadn't been prepared for, but supposedly this wasn't his first murder investigation.

Of all the suspects, Lorna seemed to have the strongest motive, plus she'd been seen in the backyard that morning. She'd lied about it, too, which made me doubly suspicious. I couldn't think of an innocent reason to be out there before dawn.

Angela, on the other hand, didn't strike me as having a compelling reason to kill Jerome. Even if he'd lied to her about leaving his wife, it didn't make a whole lot of sense to murder him. She didn't have anything to gain except revenge and I didn't get that vibe from her.

Of course, I didn't have any idea what William Wagner was going to say. He might have the strongest motive yet and make both of the women look completely innocent.

I was deep into my spreadsheets when the door cracked open and my mother stuck her head in.

"Am I interrupting anything?"

"You are and thank goodness. I've been staring at these spreadsheets for the last hour and I could use a break. Can I get you a coffee or tea?"

I started to stand but Mom shook her head and waved me back into my chair, running a finger over one of Howard's leaves. "No, I'm fine. I came by to suggest a few dates for our girls' weekend. I was hoping we could go the weekend before Thanksgiving."

Pulling up my calendar on the screen, I nodded in agreement. "That looks good, as long as all of this drama is wrapped up by then."

My mother sat back in the chair and crossed her legs. She looked stylish this morning in a pair of dark jeans and a bright red cotton sweater. Her hair appeared to be freshly washed and she was wearing makeup. Not tons of it, but just enough. She looked…young. Or younger than I'd seen her look in a long time. She also seemed happy, which made me feel about two inches tall. I did want my parents to be happy. I wasn't a horrible person normally. All of this divorce stuff had simply caught me off guard.

"I would imagine it would be soon," Mom replied. "I heard the sheriff has several suspects in custody today. It might be solved before sundown."

The gossip mill moved fast in a little town. But as usual, it had distorted a few facts.

"I don't know if I would describe them as being in custody, Mom. That's kind of a stretch."

"They're at the station. Maybe someone won't be able to take the pressure when he questions them and they'll confess."

"This isn't Perry Mason."

Tapping her chin, Peggy smiled. "Sheriff Garrett does sort of look like a Hollywood star though, doesn't he? So handsome and rugged. So…manly. You could do much worse."

Apparently, my own mother didn't think I could do any better. Nice.

"So I've been told. If you like him so much, maybe you should date him. Isn't that what you do now?"

The thought of my mother or father going out on a date horrified me in actuality. I probably shouldn't be encouraging her. She might take me up on it.

"He's a little young for me. I don't want anyone un-der….oh…forty-eight or nine."

"You'd be a cougar."

Another thought that made me cringe. Eww.

"I think that might be fun," she said with a giggle. A giggle.

My mother just giggled about younger men. Kill me now.

Rubbing at my temples, I sighed heavily. As I'd predicted this day wasn't going well.

"Maybe you should take it slow. Baby steps and all."

"You young people are so uptight. You need to loosen up. Have some fun. You don't want to be old before your time because eventually, honey, you will be old."

"You're just a ray of sunshine today. Any more wonderful news for me?"

"If it makes you feel any better, I turned down the offer that Roger and Cherie Mullaney put in. It was far too low."

They'd put in a bid? That was news. Unwelcome news. Thank goodness they were cheapskates.

"Hopefully they'll find another haunted town. We don't need a bunch of weekenders moving into Ravenmist."

"You might want to get used to it. Angela Warner has been advertising in the bigger cities trying to get them to buy country homes here. It's the wave of the future."

Angela Warner might be a cold-blooded killer and headed to prison. It would be hard to sell condos from Cell Block D.

I tapped on the keyboard, inputting the date for our girls' weekend. "I've got you in my schedule. I'm looking forward to our weekend. Do you want me to make the arrangements?"

My mother shook her head. "No need. I'll do it. It's my treat, remember?"

"I wouldn't forget a fact like that." I wanted to make things up to my mom. I'd been a real pill and she didn't deserve that.

"You look really pretty today, Mom."

Standing, she held out her arms from her sides and twirled once for me. "Thank you. I'm trying out a few looks to see what I like. I think I sort of let myself go these last few years, but I'm looking forward to our shopping trip in Chicago and some time in the spa. I might be old but I don't have to look old."

"You're not old."

"Really? You said I was old."

"I didn't mean it."

"I think you did but I'm going to let it go. I'm sure parents always look old to their children." She reached out and pushed a stray strand of hair back that had escaped my ponytail. "You could always spruce up your look too while we're in Chicago. Get a new haircut and makeup. Maybe some new clothes."

"What for?"

Had I also let myself go? There wasn't much to dress up for in our little town. Bingo on Saturday night?

"For yourself. Don't you like to feel attractive?"

I hadn't given it much thought.

"Am I unattractive?"

"Of course not. You're a Hamilton." My mom's Southern accent really showed itself at moments like this. "I was simply thinking that it might be time to change up your look. How long have you worn your hair like that? How old are those pants?"

I couldn't remember, which wasn't a good sign. Peggy might have a valid point.

"I'll think about it," I finally answered. "But I'm doing it for myself, not because I'm trying to catch a man or anything."

Peggy laughed as she breezed out of my office. "I don't think you're as done with love and men as you think you are."

I was done. Completely and totally. I'd learned my lesson. Life was better when I only had to worry about myself. And a fern.

Chapter Seventeen

TO MY SURPRISE, when I emerged from my office at lunchtime Lorna was sitting in the dining room as if everything in her world was hunky-dory. Adam was at the table as well, smiling and laughing at something Lorna had said. It must have gone well with the sheriff today.

"I don't want to wait on her."

Sighing, I turned around to see one of my waitstaff, Shelly Marbelle, holding a pitcher of water and wearing a scowl. Shelly was a good server but she wasn't the easiest of employees. She took quite a bit of time off for mysterious ailments that would have killed most people. About a year ago, I stopped Googling her diseases but they'd all been rare and strange. I still have no idea how she managed to contract curare poisoning but she seemed to have recovered completely.

"Wait on who?"

"Her." Shelly nodded toward Lorna and Adam. "She's a killer and I don't want to end up dead."

That was a mile-high jump in conclusions.

"First of all, the sheriff hasn't arrested Mrs. Bergstrom so I don't think calling her a killer is a nice thing to do. She might be innocent. There are other suspects." Shelley opened her mouth to reply but I shook my head. I wasn't done talking yet. "Secondly, even if she is the killer that doesn't mean she wants to kill you. She might just want a drink of water."

Shelly's lips tightened. "I don't want to wait on her. I don't want to be her next victim."

This conversation was going nowhere fast.

"I don't think Lorna Bergstrom is trolling the streets and alleyways of Ravenmist looking for people to kill, nor do I think she'd hack you to death in broad daylight in full view of the other diners. But if still think she's a threat, why don't you ask Sally to take her table? You can take table three."

"That's Bob Abernathy. He only tips a nickel."

Because he was about a hundred and fifty years old and that's what they tipped back then.

"The killer or the bad tipper. Those are your choices."

Grumbling, Shelly decided that it was better to be alive and have a nickel than be dead with money you couldn't spend. Sally didn't seem to have any issues waiting on Lorna and her friend so I ducked into the kitchen to see how things were going in there and to grab a bite to eat. Imagine my surprise to see the sheriff sitting at one of the counters eating a slab of lasagna from last night's dinner.

This was becoming a habit and I wasn't sure I was on board with it. Why was Garrett spending so much time here at the inn?

Oh my stars, he wasn't...sweet on me, was he? That would

be the worst. If he asked me out on a date and I turned him down I'd be getting speeding tickets every day for the rest of my life. Or until he retired, whichever came first.

"Shouldn't you be interrogating suspects instead of sucking down free food?"

I sounded unnaturally aggressive, but I was still knocked sideways seeing him for the second time today and it wasn't even one in the afternoon.

"I intend to pay for my lunch."

"Then why aren't you eating it in the dining room?"

His raised eyebrows answered the stupid question I'd asked. Lorna was in that dining room.

"I take it the questioning didn't go well then."

He took a sip of his coffee and wiped his mouth with a paper napkin. "It went great as far as I'm concerned. I learned so much today."

"Did you learn the identity of the murderer?"

"Not for sure but I have some ideas."

Glancing over at my kitchen staff, they were all pretending to be hard at work but I knew they had one ear cocked trying to listen for juicy gossip. Luckily the kitchen was almost pure mayhem and it was also incredibly loud. As long as Garrett didn't yell they wouldn't hear anything.

"You need to keep your voice down."

"Because something might actually be a secret in this town? I doubt it. I'm sure my secretary or maybe one of my deputies has already put the word out on the gossip mills about what happened this morning."

Mocking. It was the only way to describe his grin. I was in no mood for it.

"Sounds like you are beginning to get small town life."

The head chef had anticipated my appearance and he had another plate filled with lasagna and a slice of garlic bread. I had a feeling Garrett's plate had originally been mine.

I was fine with it but I wasn't comping that meal. He could pay like every other customer.

"I'm trying. Seriously, what have you heard?"

I settled into the chair next to him, digging into my lunch. The aroma of tomatoes and garlic made my stomach growl and I realized it had been hours since I'd last eaten.

"I haven't heard anything. I've been working all morning. I did see Lorna and Adam eating lunch on the way in here. She doesn't look upset. Did she get a better alibi?"

Because her original one was a big, fat lie. The sheriff just didn't know it.

"No, but then no one seems to have a decent alibi in this group. Everybody was sleeping, which makes logical sense but it doesn't make for a great alibi."

I took a big bite of my lasagna. So delicious. "So what did they say?"

I didn't think he'd answer, although he'd said that the grapevine would be buzzing already.

"Why should I tell you?"

"Maybe because you're sitting in my kitchen eating my food.

Clearly, you came here for a reason."

"I might just have been hungry."

"Then you could have gone to Daisy's."

"She keeps wanting to read my palm."

"She's psychic."

"How charming. Too bad she can't tell that I don't want my fortune told."

Garrett was a laugh a minute. Bet he wasn't much fun at parties.

"So are you going to tell me or not? I could go ask Daisy or someone else but then I might get the wrong story. The rumor mill isn't much for getting the details right, Sheriff."

Wadding up the paper napkin, Garrett tucked it under the edge of his now empty plate. "I kind of did come here on purpose."

Victory tasted sweet. I would have done a lap around the kitchen to thunderous applause and inspiring music but we were in the middle of the lunch rush. Perhaps later.

"You wanted my opinion."

"I did not want your opinion."

"Then why are you here?"

"Lunch."

"You're done. You can leave at any time."

Except that I didn't want him to. I wanted him to talk.

"For an innkeeper you're lousy at hospitality."

"You're not a guest."

"What did you do before this? Let me guess… you worked at

the DMV. You've got the personality for it. I bet you were employee of the month more than once."

"I was a senior researcher for a financial institution."

"Sounds fancy."

"It was boring but it paid well. I'm extremely detail-oriented. Now are you going to tell me what they said or do I have to torture it out of you?"

Barking with laughter at the mere idea, Garrett grinned. "Torture? How do you plan to do that?"

"I'll eat a slice of deep dish apple pie right in front of you but I won't let them serve you any."

His smile faded. "You wouldn't."

"I would."

I already knew that he loved my pastry chef's apple pie. Just last week he'd scarfed down a gigantic slice in record time. I'd never seen anything like it before.

"With ice cream?"

"You bet. I'd heat it up and have ice cream. Two scoops."

"No, I mean I want ice cream with it. If I'm going to spill the beans I'm going to need compensation."

I ran my gaze up and down, from his toes to his forehead. He was a good-looking man. But ornery.

"You'll ruin your girlish figure."

"I'll take my chances."

"Don't move. I'll get your pie and then you'll talk. Right, Garrett?"

"Right. Two scoops." He paused before continuing. "And

Tedi? Call me Jack."

"Are we becoming friends?"

"Worse things could happen. As weird as you are, you're the most sane person in this crazy town."

What a sweet talker. I'd take it as a compliment because I think he meant it as one. In a backhanded sort of way.

"Friends," I repeated, pondering what that might be like. "I guess we could try it."

The idea suddenly didn't seem so far-fetched.

HE SHOVED THE last mouthful of apple-goodness into his mouth and closed his eyes in what appeared to be a food heaven euphoria.

"So Lorna didn't have much more to say?"

"No, she admitted that she and Roger are having an affair but she claims that she and Jerome had an understanding. Sort of an open marriage kind of thing. He had his dalliances and she had hers. They weren't going to divorce over it. She said she had no reason to kill her husband."

"Did they have a prenup? That would be reason to kill him."

"They did, which makes her claim a stretch of imagination. As far as I'm concerned, she's still a suspect. But not my strongest one."

"Wagner?"

Garrett – no, Jack – had already said that the two men had

argued because Wagner accused Jerome of stealing from the consulting company they both owned. Jerome denied it but Wagner had threatened to go to the police. Money was a powerful motive for murder and the businessman didn't have a strong alibi. Like so many others, he'd been asleep in his hotel room in Travistown. No witnesses.

"Angela."

That I hadn't expected. She had the weakest motive from what I could see, but then I wasn't an experienced cop.

"Angela? How is she your strongest suspect?"

"Wagner said that Jerome talked about her quite a bit. How he was stringing her along with promises to leave Lorna but he wasn't planning on doing it. Then he said that Jerome was thinking about ending things since she was getting clingy. He might even have done it. Wagner wasn't sure."

"They looked pretty chummy the night of the festival."

"They certainly did," Jack agreed. "But from that distance we couldn't tell if he was kissing her or she was kissing him. Just how *mutual* that clinch was is up in the air."

"He came here to Ravenmist," I pointed out. "He must have wanted to see her."

"Or he wanted her to see him with his wife. According to Wagner, Jerome wasn't a nice guy. He was a real jerk and he wouldn't put it past his partner to be that vindictive."

"And yet he still shared a business with him. Lie down with dogs, you get up with fleas," I quoted, remembering my mother saying the very same thing when I was younger.

Jack smiled and shook his head. "I haven't heard that in years but it's true. If Jerome was stealing it shouldn't have come as a shock."

"Where does that leave Adam, Roger, and Cherie? Are they cleared?"

"I don't have any reason to suspect them," Jack shrugged taking the last bite of the fast-melting ice cream. "Do you know something I don't?"

I did but it didn't have anything to do with those three. I wanted to tell him about Lorna not being in bed but I still didn't know how. At the moment it was going to have to be enough that she was still under suspicion.

"I just wondered," I said instead. "Did you know Roger and Cherie are looking for a house in town? They made an offer on my parents' place but it was too low."

The gossip train must not stop in front of the police station. I'd surprised the sheriff. Go me.

"They are? I had no idea." His expression softened. "I heard about your parents. I'm sorry to hear about their marriage."

"I just want them to be happy," I said automatically. Because I did. But I still wasn't thrilled by how they were going about it. "I'm just surprised Roger and Cherie want to put down roots in a community where one of their good friends was brutally murdered. Seems strange to me."

"It wouldn't be my first choice, but if Bergstrom was anything at all like how he's been described by everyone who knew him they might not care that he's dead."

"So what now?"

"After all of that food? A nap would be nice."

Jack could be charming. Interesting. Did I dare trust him enough to be friends?

"Seriously, you can't take a nap with a killer on the loose."

"No, I can't, which is a shame. I need to talk to Angela again now that I've talked to Wagner. See what she has to say."

"Is this how police work usually goes? You just keep talking to people until someone confesses or the crime lab gives you a clue?"

Laughing, Jack pushed his empty plate away. "I guess that's how it might look from the outside but I can assure you there is quite a bit going on in the background. Lorna's prenup, Bergstrom's business, Angela's phone and text messages. I'm putting together a puzzle. One piece at a time."

I'd never liked jigsaw puzzles when I was a kid but later as a researcher I'd learned that puzzles could be fun. But this one? It was a real killer. Too many suspects and few clues. Jack had his hands full trying to crack this case.

Chapter Eighteen

ROGER AND CHERIE Mullaney were standing in the middle of the living room of the house that Angela had insisted I look at. She'd decided that it was "perfect" for me and I had to admit she might be right. She had great taste in houses. This one was an adorable three-bedroom Craftsman with tons of curb appeal.

But I wasn't all that fond of the furnishings if the Mullaneys came with the house.

With an evil grin, Roger put his arm around Cherie. "Looks like we might have some competition for this one, honey. We didn't realize you were looking for a house too, Tedi."

"I'm looking for more privacy than I get at the inn."

Cherie nodded sympathetically. "I can imagine that must be exhausting, being on call twenty-hour hours a day."

"It's not that bad and I'm used to it." I trailed my fingers down the edge of a bookcase that banked the fireplace. "But I'm thinking about a change."

"It's a lovely home," Cherie enthused, her gaze running around the room. "But we were hoping for a bigger yard. I like to garden. Your parents' home was perfect."

Were they planning on putting in a higher offer? I didn't ask. I'd grown up in a family where we didn't talk about money. It had been drilled into us that it was gauche and rude. It was hard enough talking to Angela about it and she was a professional.

"It is a great house," I agreed. "But a lot of maintenance for something that large."

"We'd hire someone to do that," Cherie dismissed. "The back yard is perfect for a huge garden and maybe a pool."

A pool? They wanted to put in a pool? That was my childhood dream but my parents had only laughed and told me it wasn't practical. We could only use it a few months a year. Maybe Roger and Cherie could adopt me. How did they feel about ponies and a carousel?

Roger shook Angela's hand. "Thank you for showing us the house. We'll give it some serious thought."

"I think it could be a great second home for you."

The couple said their goodbyes and exited the house, leaving me with Angela. I wanted to know what she was thinking after being questioned by Garre – no, Jack, this morning. I was going to need to get used to that. We were friends now.

Angela waved out of the front window as the Mullaneys drove away. "Such a nice couple. But I think they'd be happier in your family's home. I think this house is better for you, Tedi."

Then she'd make two commissions.

"Did you know Roger Mullaney before the weekend?" I asked, checking out the built-in cabinets in the dining room.

They were amazing. I didn't need a house but I kind of wanted this one already.

"At the festival," Angela said. "He seemed okay. Typical city person. Now what do you think of these built-in bookshelves?"

The workmanship was top notch. I would know, too, as my dad liked to refinish old furniture as a hobby. He would love this house. If I didn't buy it, he might be interested in it since he and Mom were going to sell theirs.

Divorce. I ruthlessly pushed it from my brain, not ready to deal with it yet. My mother had always loved Scarlett O'Hara so I'd take a page out of her book and think about it tomorrow.

The master bedroom was huge and the closets were even a decent size. The kitchen had been renovated recently, and although I wasn't the biggest fan of stainless steel – fingerprints, folks – I had to admit the house was as Angela had promised…perfect.

"You met Roger at the festival? Since he was such a good friend of Jerome Bergstrom's I thought you might have met him before."

I had to focus and remember why I was here. I was blinded by marble countertops and a steam shower.

"No, I don't think so. Jerome and I liked to stay in when I was in the city."

The laundry room was a little small but I couldn't have everything I wanted. "How did you meet him?"

I wasn't all that sly or stealthy. Angela had to realize she was being pumped for information but she must have really wanted to make this sale because she didn't call me on my terrible sleuthing skills.

"At a friend's cocktail party. Her boyfriend had some business dealings with Jerome." Her expression grew sad, her lips drooping down. "He was really wonderful to me."

"He seemed a little…abrasive."

"He could be but with me he was a teddy bear."

As hard as I might try, I couldn't imagine Jerome as a teddy bear. Not even close. I opened my mouth to ask another question but Angela was still talking.

"His wife killed him." She slapped the top of the kitchen counter, making a loud sound in the quiet. "I know she did. She hated Jerome and treated him terribly. She only married him for his money. I'm shocked they stayed together as long as they did, frankly. Jerry told me some stories from their marriage and let me tell you, Tedi, she's a horrible woman. She definitely did it."

"Do you have any evidence of it? If so, I hope you told the sheriff."

"I told him all of the things that Jerry told me but the sheriff said that it was hearsay and not admissible in court."

This was my chance.

"Did it go okay? When you talked to the sheriff?"

"It was fine. He asked about our relationship and what Jerry promised me. I told him the truth. He asked if he could see our emails and texts and I said absolutely he could. I have nothing to hide."

"What about William Wagner?"

Angela shrugged. "What about him? From what Jerry told me his partner is always screaming about something. Overemotional is how he described him."

"So you don't think he killed Jerome?"

"No," Angela said firmly. "Lorna definitely did it. For the money. If Wagner killed Jerry, what would he gain? Nothing. No, it was Lorna."

As quickly as Angela had turned serious she brightened up, her smile blinding. "So what do you think of the house? It's perfect, isn't it?"

"I have to admit it is."

I didn't need a house. Did I? This place was everything I'd ever wanted in a home and then some.

"Should I draw up an offer?"

"Give me a little time to take all of this in." It was moving a little too fast for me. "I didn't think you'd find one this quickly."

Or at all. I'd given Angela the pickiest criteria I could so that it wouldn't be bizarre when I gave up house hunting in defeat.

"Okay, but don't wait too long. A gem like this is going to be scooped up fast. Roger and Cherie are interested and the price is right. You don't want to miss out."

I didn't but I also didn't want to jump into anything without looking first. It was a big decision. Plus, there was Terrence to think about.

He was the ghost in my life, and I didn't want him to be lonely.

"TERRENCE," I CALLED when I entered my bedroom. "Are you around? Can you hear me?"

I tossed my purse on the bed and stuck my head into the open walk-in closet. I never closed the door anymore. It felt rude. I figured he could close it if he wanted a little privacy.

Speaking of privacy... I'd taken to getting dressed in the en suite bathroom. The horse might be out of the barn but it made me feel better.

"Of course, I can hear you. I'm dead, not deaf."

"I wasn't sure. You might have gone somewhere."

"Where would I go?" Terrence still hadn't shown himself but I had hopes that eventually he would trust me enough. *"I don't know anyone but you."*

"I don't know. Maybe you could cruise around town and see what's going on. I know you like to people watch."

"There's people here."

This didn't bode well for talking him into leaving the inn.

"You don't ever want to see how the town looks now? It's grown but I bet it's still the same in many ways."

"I like it here."

Sighing, I set the chair in front of the door again. Terrence didn't want to go into the light and he didn't want to leave my closet.

"What if you had a better home? With your own room? Wouldn't you like that?"

There was silence and I waited, holding my breath for his answer.

"I don't know," he replied, slowly appearing in front of me along with a chilly breeze that ran over my skin. He was younger than I'd imagined, perhaps around eighteen or nineteen. His dark hair was clipped short and he was dressed in trousers and a white button-down shirt. A surge of happiness ran through my veins at his appearance. He'd actually showed himself. To me. And yes, I did feel darn special right at the moment. *"Would there be people there, too?"*

Don't make a big deal out of it. Act natural.

"Well…not like here."

The house was in a quiet area by design. With a sinking heart, I realized that Terrence wouldn't like it. He wouldn't have anyone to watch but maybe a few deer and some squirrels in the backyard.

"Why would I want to leave here? It's great here. I have everything I need."

There was more silence and I decided to table the discussion. If I hadn't made up my mind there was no point in upsetting Terrence.

"It is great here. So, what did you do today?"

"You're selling the inn, aren't you? I figured this day would come."

I'd handled this badly. I was supposed to be a people person but you would never know it by this fiasco. "No, I'm not. Not at all. I love this inn and I can't imagine ever wanting to sell it."

"Then why are you asking me about moving?"

There was suspicion in his tone so I decided to come clean. I'd already screwed this up royally.

"I looked at a house today and I really liked it. I haven't made any decisions," I said hastily. "I wasn't even really looking to move but I have to admit that the house is fantastic. I just...well...if I go I'd want you to go with me. You know, if you wanted to."

As quickly as he'd appeared, he disappeared into the wall. The only sign I hadn't imagined the whole thing was the puff of cool air that accompanied his entrance and exits. There was no answer to my question and I waited a long time, the minutes ticking by slowly. My stomach twisted into a painful knot as I sat there hoping he would answer me. After ten minutes or so, I gave up. Standing, I placed the chair back against the wall.

I'd messed it all up. Terrence hated me.

It had only been a few days but already I'd grown quite fond of the young man in my closet. Only a voice but we'd shared something precious. My Grandma Rose.

I'd try and talk to him again tomorrow. I was walking toward the bathroom when he finally spoke, making me jump with surprise, although his tone was softer than normal.

"Thank you, Tedi. Your offer is nice but I think that I'd rather stay here. This is my home."

I couldn't argue with that and I didn't try. My throat was tight at the mere thought of leaving my new friend. Square footage and big windows were nice but they couldn't replace what I had here.

"Good night, Terrence. Sweet dreams."

"Good night, Tedi. See you in the morning."

I wasn't going to buy that house.

Chapter Nineteen

I'D BARELY DRAGGED myself out of bed when my phone started chiming and lighting up. Missy's ringtone. It must be important to be calling me so early in the morning. She knew I needed at least two cups of coffee before I liked talking to people.

"Decent people don't call this early."

I could hear Missy's snort through the phone.

"If you want me not to tell you my news, then I'll hang up while you caffeinate. Your choice."

"I want the news."

I just wanted it an hour from now.

"I ushered Roger Mullaney's soul into the light about twenty minutes ago. He was murdered in the house you looked at yesterday."

In my shock, I lost hold of the phone and dropped it onto the maple flooring with a loud clatter. I muttered a few words that my mother wouldn't have approved of and quickly picked it up, hoping I hadn't lost Missy, too.

"Sorry. So sorry," I said immediately, pressing the phone to my ear. "I dropped the phone. Are you serious? Are you sure it was Roger?"

"I kind of have to be sure, Tedi. I can't go around harvesting souls willy nilly. They frown on that. I have to fill out a heck of a lot of paperwork so I have to know who is who. It was Roger and boy, was he upset that he was dead. He was madder than a wet hen. He practically stomped into the light saying that he was glad he was dead and anyplace had to be better than this."

"Did you ask him who the killer was?" I asked, excited that we might finally have broken the case. If Roger named his murderer, chances are we'd know who killed Jerome, too.

Except that I had no clue why anyone would want to murder Roger. It didn't make any sense. This was two murders in our little town in less than a week. It was unprecedented and I hoped it wasn't a trend. That could really hurt tourism.

"I didn't have to ask him. He'd...written the name on the wall. Where he found a pen in that empty house I have no idea."

I did. There had been several felt tip pens next to the sign-in sheet for the open house. If he was close enough, he could have grabbed any one of them.

Focus. He named his killer. This isn't about pens.

"What name did he write?"

"Lorna. Well...almost. He wrote the L-O-R before he expired."

"Did you call the sheriff?"

"Of course, I did, Tedi." Missy's tone was a tad sarcastic. "As soon as I got the page, I changed into my reaper robes, guided his soul into the light, and then called the sheriff to let him know. We had coffee and donuts together while I told him all about my cool hobby with dead people."

"You could have just said it was a stupid question."

"It was a stupid question."

"What I meant was did you maybe make an anonymous call to 911 or something?"

Another heavy sigh. "We both know that Ida is on the switchboard this morning and she'd recognize my voice."

That was true. Living in a small town had its blessings and its curses.

"So he doesn't know?"

"Not as of twenty minutes ago."

Jack needed to know but I didn't know how to tell him. Like Terrence seeing Lorna the morning that Jerome was killed, I couldn't tell him that a supernatural entity had given me the information.

"Maybe I could call Angela and tell her I want to see the house again. Then we can *discover* Roger."

"That's a good idea. Can you act shocked and surprised?"

"I'm a veritable Meryl Streep."

"Right. Okay, well give her a call. The sheriff isn't going to find out until someone walks into that house."

I hung up with Missy but hadn't put down my phone. It was early. Really early in the morning, the sun barely up. It would be weird to call Angela at this hour, no matter how much she might think I want that house.

I'll shower first. Then I'll call. Roger – the poor man – wasn't going anywhere.

I SENT ANGELA a text as soon as it was a decent hour to do so but she didn't answer, which was weird. Normally she was right there, responding within seconds but I waited for twenty minutes and nothing. I triple checked that the text had actually been sent and then sent another one, but still no answer. I decided to drive to her office, hoping that she was okay. We'd had a rash of dead bodies in this town and I didn't want my real estate agent to be one of them. She didn't have any connection to Roger, but Lorna didn't seem to be too fond of her.

Lorna. I really hadn't thought she was the one. I didn't know anything about killers but I hadn't gotten that feeling from her. Looks like I couldn't trust my gut instincts when it came to murder.

I didn't get as far as the door, however. Jack strode into my lobby, almost mowing down a nice old gentleman who was looking for the local paper. From the set of his jaw and shoulders I had a feeling that I didn't need to see that house again. Someone had already discovered Roger's body.

I needed to act shocked. I wasn't supposed to know about this.

"Jack, to what do we owe the honor?"

"I need to speak to Cherie Mullaney and also Lorna Bergstrom."

Act casual. You know nothing.

"I haven't seen either one of them in the dining room for breakfast yet. Is it important?"

Hooking his thumbs in his belt, Garrett's eyes narrowed. "I would think so. Roger Mullaney is dead."

Roger was dead. Deceased. Passed on. Not alive. Jack certainly hadn't sugarcoated it.

Missy had already told me but this was confirmation. Not that I thought she would lie to me but the whole Grim Reaper thing was still sort of surreal at this point.

And Lorna was the killer. It still didn't make much sense to me. I could see her wanting Jerome dead but Roger? If they'd been having an affair why did she murder him? My head hurt from all of the unanswered questions.

"Are you listening to me?"

Not as closely as I should have been.

"Yes, I am but there's a lot going on here this morning."

What with people dying and one of my guests being a murderer…

"Is there another murder I need to know about?"

I didn't think so but these days anything could happen. The town had gone crazy.

"I would hope not," I said in a huffy tone. "I'll go find Cherie and Lorna. Maybe they slept in."

"I'll wait in the drawing room. I need to speak to Cherie undisturbed, and then I'll speak with Lorna."

Because she was the killer. Roger had said so with his last dying breath. Sort of.

"I'll go find Cherie first." I paused before heading upstairs. Would he tell me? "Who do you think did it?"

"I can't really discuss that, Tedi. Can you get Cherie now?"

"I'll go find Cherie. You can drop into the kitchen and get some coffee and breakfast if you like. I doubt you've had time for any."

His features softened and he actually looked grateful. "That would be good. Thank you."

This friendship might work out after all.

But first he had to arrest Lorna Bergstrom and tell Cheri Mullaney her husband was dead.

Chapter Twenty

CRYING WOMEN IN my drawing room were becoming a terrible habit. This time it was Cherie sobbing into a box of tissues while Jack paced back and forth asking questions.

This time, however, I wasn't hiding in the closet listening. I was hovering in the doorway ready to deliver news that wasn't going to make the sheriff happy in the least. Jack was asking questions and Cherie was tearfully answering them. Her story was that she'd been tucked up in bed all night and hadn't even realized Roger had left their bed.

That sounded familiar. Who had said that? Right…Lorna.

"Do you know why he might do that?" the sheriff asked. "Does he do that often?"

Cherie sniffled into her tissue. "Lorna must have lured him there."

Apparently, she'd been told about Roger's last dying message.

Jack stopped his pacing, his fingers rubbing at his temple. He looked uncomfortable. "Mrs. Mullaney, did you know about your husband and Lorna Bergstrom?"

Dabbing at damp cheeks, Cherie nodded. "He told me not long ago. He said they were done and he wasn't going to see her anymore. That's why we were looking for a house here in Ravenmist. Sort of a new start. We both thought a weekend home in the country would be nice. It's what we'd talked about for years."

I'd been married in the past, folks. I must tell you that I would have been hard pressed to go on a couples weekend with my husband's ex-fling. I wouldn't care that it was over. I would care that he'd had an affair with a woman who was supposed to be my best friend. I wasn't the type for a catfight but I sure wouldn't be all chummy with her either.

"Yet you came here with Lorna and Jerome this weekend," I said before I could stop myself. Jack and Cherie hadn't even known I was standing there and now I was asking questions. "She had an affair with your husband. You're a much nicer person than I am."

Scowling, Jack shot me a warning look that said I'd be hearing about my transgression. I was out of line but my mouth sometimes ran ahead of my good judgment.

"Tedi, I'll ask the questions here." He turned back to Cherie. "But it's actually not a bad one. You don't think it's strange to travel with your husband's ex-mistress?"

"The vacation was planned months ago. After this I would only have to see them at social events where we were both invited. Besides, I loved and trusted Roger. If he said it was over, it was over." More sobs from Cherie, her shoulders shaking with their force. "We came here for a vacation and look what's happened. This town is cursed."

Cheric probably wouldn't be buying my parents' home anymore. She wouldn't want to settle down in a town where two husbands had been murdered.

Both husbands? Seriously, what were the odds? They had to be astronomical.

"Tedi, did you need something?"

I was pulled from my reverie by Jack's sharp tone.

"Yes. I need to speak with you."

"Unless it's important—"

"It's important."

He sighed heavily and gave me another look. I was definitely going to hear about it when we were alone.

"Will you excuse me for a moment, Mrs. Mullaney? I'll be right back." He followed me out of the drawing room and into the hallway. "Tedi, I'm working. You cannot just waltz in there—"

"I can't find Lorna."

That stopped Jack in his tracks. His eyes widened and he took a minute before replying.

"What do you mean you can't *find* her?"

"I can't find her. Or Adam Taylor, her attorney. They're both not in their rooms or anywhere on the grounds. My front desk clerk said she saw them walk out of the inn about a half hour ago. I checked the parking lot and Adam's car is gone."

"They're gone?" Jack growled. "They walked out and left?"

"If it helps, all of their stuff is still in their rooms. Maybe they just went out for breakfast."

"That doesn't help. We have to find them. I'll put a BOLO out for the vehicle."

He pulled his phone from his pocket and barked orders into, presumably to some poor deputy back at the station. When he finished his call, he tucked it away again and moved to head back into the drawing room. But...

"Jack, did you ever see the movie *Strangers on a Train*?"

He paused, his brows drawn down into a scowl. "Are you asking me out on a date?"

He really did have a healthy ego. We were friends and that's all. I was still getting used to not being annoyed by him.

"Heavens to Betsy, no. I'm asking you if you've seen the movie."

He shrugged and sighed heavily. "Maybe. I don't know. If I did it wasn't memorable. Do we have to talk about this now?"

"You'd remember if you saw it. It's an Alfred Hitchcock film starring Farley Granger and Robert Walker. An old black and white."

The only kind of movies I watched when I was taking a break from baking shows.

Rubbing the back of his neck, he shifted impatiently on his feet. "Can you get to the point here? I'm kind of in the middle of something."

"I'm trying. It's about two people who meet on a train. I won't go into detail–"

"Thank you," Garrett interrupted, his arms crossed over his

chest.

"But basically, they decide to switch murders. They both want someone to be eliminated from their lives so Robert Walker suggests that they each murder the other's problem person. That way they'd never get caught because they have no connection to the victim. Farley Granger thinks it's all a joke and agrees but doesn't think that it's actually going to happen. Robert Walker, on the other hand, thinks he's perfectly serious and goes and does the murder. Then he pressures Farley Granger into killing his problem person. They made a deal, after all."

"And?"

I rolled my eyes and groaned. "Can't you see it?"

"Pretend I can't." He checked his watch. "And make it fast because Mrs. Mullaney is waiting for me."

"What if Lorna and Cherie are Robert Walker and Farley Granger?"

"Then they're the dumbest criminals on the planet. They'd be the first suspects and they haven't alibied each other. Sleeping is not an alibi. The movie sounds really interesting and I think I should rent it, but I don't think Lorna and Cherie came to Ravenmist to kill each other's husbands. If they did, they should have worked on the plan a little longer. It sucks."

I threw up my hands in frustration. "The probability of both their husbands being murdered has to be a billion to one. Don't you think it's odd?"

He leaned down so we were almost nose to nose. "Of course, I do. You're absolutely right, the odds are out of the stratosphere.

But you're forgetting one thing. We already know who the murderer is. Mullaney told us. Lorna Bergstrom."

"She might have killed him but that doesn't mean she killed Jerome."

Although Terrence had seen her walking around early that morning. That detail was still not known by Jack.

"The knife wounds were similar, although I don't have all the details. The state lab is running more tests. I'll ask this question. Do you have reason to believe that this is a *Strangers on a Train* scenario, other than you watch too many old movies?"

"No," I admitted. "It just seemed strange."

"This whole town is strange. Can I go now?"

"Yes, you can go. I was just trying to help."

"I know and stop it. Investigating a murder isn't for amateurs and it can be dangerous. Stick to running the inn, okay?"

What could I say? I had to agree.

"Okay, I let the professionals handle it."

"Thank you. Now if you really want to help me, keep an eye out for Lorna Bergstrom and Adam Taylor. If they return, call me."

If Lorna Bergstrom killed her husband, she'd be an idiot to come back.

Chapter Twenty-One

I TRIED TO concentrate on spreadsheets and purchase orders but my thoughts kept drifting back to Lorna, Cherie, Jerome, and Roger. Adam too, although I wasn't sure just what role he played in all of this mess. The whole situation was bad on so many levels I couldn't see how Jack was going to make any sense out of it.

Finally, I gave up and sent a text to Missy to meet me at Daisy's for a late lunch. The special today was chicken and dumplings. I didn't want to miss it.

The cafe wasn't far so I pulled on a pair of gloves to go along with my coat and headed down Maple. The weather was sunny but crisp, a perfect autumn day. The town center was bustling as usual with shoppers and tourists checking out the funky antique shops. I waved to Chet who owned the newsstand and Sandy who ran the beauty shop. Both places were good for gossip but everyone in Ravenmist knew that the best stories could be found at Daisy's. Some of it was even true.

As I passed the sheriff's station I glanced into the big window in the front and was shocked to see Lorna and Adam in handcuffs. Both of them were sitting on a bench outside Jack's office and Lorna's eyes were red and swollen from crying.

Two sides of me warred as I stood there on the cold sidewalk and took in the sad scene. Part of me felt sorry for the widow and the trouble she'd found herself in. She might not have been happy with her husband but she probably didn't want him dead. The other half of me said that she absolutely did want him dead and she'd killed him. My sympathy was misplaced. I didn't know Lorna well at all, so I shouldn't be making judgments about whether she was a killer or not. She might be the best person in the world or she might be the worst. Like most people, she was probably somewhere in between.

It really depended on how far she was either way, didn't it?

Missy was waiting for me in the café, sipping an iced tea and chatting with Daisy. I slid into the other side of the booth and breathlessly apologized for being late.

"I saw Lorna and Adam in handcuffs," I confessed, tugging off my gloves. "I guess they found them."

Daisy nodded knowingly. "They certainly did. They were on the highway headed out of town when the state police pulled them over."

"How do you know all of that already?" I marveled. "Lorna and Adam still had their coats on. They couldn't have been at the station all that long."

"Helen stopped by to pick up some lunch for the rest of the station house," Daisy said with a smirk. "She filled me in while the kitchen made up the order."

Helen Calhoun was Jack's administrative assistant and at least eighty-five if she was a day. She'd been the assistant to the sheriff since I was a little kid and probably rode a dinosaur to work at one point. Jack had been encouraging her to retire since he'd taken the job of sheriff.

Because of her long tenure, she also had delusions of grandeur and would go around town doing little "citizen arrests" when people were double parked or they crossed against the light. Most of the town's folk humored her but it had been getting worse lately and she was liable to end up run over by a UPS truck if she didn't stop.

Why a UPS truck, you ask?

A couple of months ago, one had been parked in front of the sheriff's station while the driver dropped off some packages at a nearby business. Helen had decided she didn't like that so she climbed into the driver's seat and tried to re-park the hulking vehicle. She'd scraped four parked cars and rear-ended a deputy before Jack had stopped her.

Come to think of it, that had been Jack's first week on the job. Welcome to Ravenmist.

"Jack is going to blow a gasket," I said. "He hates the rumor mill in town."

"He might have to finally force Helen to retire," Daisy replied. "Her memory is starting to go, you know. The entire time she was here she kept calling him Sheriff Woods. He retired thirty-five years ago."

"So what did Helen say?" Missy asked impatiently. "How

did they find them?"

Daisy leaned down as if to tell us a secret but I knew that everyone in town would know whatever she was telling us by sundown. "I'm not sure but they were driving on the highway out of town. Their story is that they were going to visit a friend."

The story was pretty lame. Things didn't look good for Lorna. Or Adam. That explained the handcuffs and Lorna's tearstained visage.

"That's awful," Missy said. "Just terrible."

"On the bright side, the killers are caught," Daisy said knowingly, a big smile on her face. "But I knew they would be. I had a vision last night. Sheriff Jack locking up the murderer. I couldn't see his or her face but I knew he'd get them soon. I had a vision about you, too."

She was looking at me. What now?

"A vision? What was it?"

Frankly, I wasn't sure if I really wanted to know but I wasn't going to stop Daisy from telling me. When she had one of her visions, she was going to talk about it.

"Saw you in a white wedding dress walking down an aisle."

I visibly shuddered at the thought, pictures of my wedding flashing in front of my eyes as if I was on my deathbed. Never again.

"You must be mistaken, Daisy. That wasn't me. Maybe it was Missy. She and Dylan might get married someday."

Rolling her eyes, Missy gave me a little kick under the table.

"No, it was you. Your mama and daddy were there, too. You

had one of them long trains and a big poufy veil."

There was nothing in my fashion history that said I was going to wear anything poufy. No, no, no.

"If I ever get married again – and that's a huge if – I won't be wearing a white dress. I'll just go down to the courthouse and get married by the judge. No fuss. You've mixed me up with someone else or maybe you're having memories of my sister Hyacinth's wedding. She had a big poufy dress and veil. What is it you said, Missy? She looked like a giant roll of toilet paper. The fluffy, expensive kind."

My best friend had her hand clapped over her mouth and was trying to hold in her laughter. We both had some fun memories of that day. Missy and I had been twenty at the time, a few months underage for alcohol but there had been this champagne fountain and when no one was looking…

Needless to say, we had a marvelous time at the reception and danced to every single song. We danced as if no one watching, if you get my drift. The next day we'd both had a horrible champagne hangover but tried to pretend that we were fine while taking turns throwing up in the hall bathroom of my childhood home.

My mother, of course, figured out that we were sick and blamed it on the shrimp cocktail. To this day, she won't let me eat shellfish when I'm with her because she says I must be *allergic*.

"It wasn't Hyacinth. It was you, and you were getting married. Might as well get used to the idea. The right man will change your mind."

"If I find the right man, then I'll keep an open mind. How does that sound?"

"It sounds like you're pacifying me but I'll let you. Now what do you want for lunch?"

"Chicken and dumplings," I answered immediately. "And iced tea. No lemon."

Daisy made a face and scribbled down my order. "As if I don't know how you take your tea by now. I should have known you'd want my special chicken and dumplings. The recipe is a secret."

They really were the best I'd ever tasted, and I'd tried to duplicate the recipe many times but had never been able to.

"Someday I'll figure out the secret ingredient."

"Doubtful."

"It's love, isn't it?" Missy piped up. "That's what makes it special."

"It's definitely not love. I've made that dish when I was in the worst mood in the world. Try again."

Missy wrinkled her nose. "Cilantro?"

"Perish the thought. Do you want the same?"

Missy nodded and we handed our unneeded menus to Daisy who bustled back to the kitchen, leaving us alone at the table. The restaurant was packed, the lunch rush in full swing.

"You're not thinking about that wedding dress thing, are you?" Missy asked as a waitress dropped off my tea. "Daisy isn't always right."

"No, that's not it. I was thinking about Lorna and Adam."

Missy sighed. "You've got that look on your face. What's this one about?"

"They left town and they weren't supposed to. Come on, Missy. You have to admit that it's a dumb thing to do."

"It is, but are criminals super smart?"

"I would imagine a few are and some are stupid. But that just doesn't make any sense to me. Plus, what is Adam's part in all of this? Lorna wasn't having an affair with him."

"That we know of," Missy interjected. "Maybe she was tired of Roger and decided to go with Adam."

"Maybe. It just bothers me when it doesn't make sense."

When I'd been researching companies in my past career, I'd always pay close attention when things didn't make sense. That's when I'd look harder. I'd usually find something that wasn't quite what it was supposed to be.

"You think she's innocent?"

Did I? I wasn't sure.

There was evidence against Lorna. Terrence had seen her wandering around the morning of her husband's murder. She wasn't happy in her marriage and she'd been having an affair. Now she'd been caught heading out of town.

"I don't know," I admitted with a sigh. "I just don't know. She had motive and opportunity, but she isn't the only one. And why would she kill Roger? That doesn't make any sense, either."

"Are you back to the *Strangers on a Train* thing? Because that only works if Lorna and Cherie were strangers. They're best friends."

I'd told Missy about my theory via text and she'd thought as much of it as Jack had. Which was not much at all.

"I know that, too. It's just this entire situation is so bizarre. It doesn't make any sense," I repeated.

"Not everything makes sense. We should just be glad that a murderer is off the streets of Ravenmist. We can get back to normal."

This town hadn't been normal in two hundred years. I wasn't even sure what that meant anymore. But my friend was right about one thing…some things simply don't make sense. I needed to leave it alone.

Chapter Twenty-Two

B Y THE TIME I returned to the inn, it appeared that everyone had heard about Lorna and Adam. The place was buzzing with conjecture about why they did it and how many other people they might have killed. This time tomorrow, Lorna and Adam would be merciless serial killers who were headed out on a nationwide rampage like Bonnie and Clyde.

I retreated to my room and kicked off my dressy shoes, placing them inside of the closet. I hoped that Terrence was around. I hadn't talked to him yet today and I was becoming quite fond of him. He had a fun sense of humor and terrific stories about my grandmother and father. He didn't talk much about himself though, and I had the feeling that his childhood hadn't been all that wonderful. Every time I tried to steer the conversation to him he'd change the subject.

"Terrence," I called out. "Are you there?"

A cold breeze ran over me and then he was standing there, wearing the same slacks and buttoned-down shirt. I made a mental note to ask him or Edward whether they were stuck for an eternity wearing whatever clothes they'd died in. If that was the case, I needed to up my wardrobe game.

"I'm here. I was out earlier though, taking a walk in the back-yard. The inn is very busy today."

"It's Halloween," I reminded him. "It's practically a national holiday in Ravenmist."

He made a face and leaned against the doorway to the closet. *"I never liked Halloween much. I don't like wearing costumes."*

"I'm okay with the costumes but I love the candy. I also love the decorations."

I'd kept up most of the Halloween decorations from the festival but tomorrow they would all come down. I was sort of sad to see the end but then I had the holiday season to look forward to.

Terrence grinned, looking rather boyish. *"I love candy. I wish I could still eat it."*

"Do you miss food?"

I would totally miss food. And soaking in a hot tub.

"Sometimes, but I don't think about it much. I don't get hungry or tired, and time doesn't work the same way it did before."

Before. I'd noticed that Terrence never referred to himself as deceased. It was always just about the *before*. Funny, but now my life was split into before and after, too. Before I knew about ghosts and the after.

"Terrence, are you sure you saw Lorna Bergstrom that morn-ing that her husband was killed? You're absolutely positive that it was her?"

Terrence frowned, his brows pulled down. *"I think so. It was from a distance but it looked like her. I could be wrong, though. Why?"*

Sighing, I sat down on the edge of the bed. "I just wondered. She and her friend are in jail right now."

"I heard."

That made me laugh. "The gossip mill even works for spirits. Good to know."

"I overheard some conversations in the dining room. It sounds like they have evidence. It's good that she's caught and behind bars, right?"

It was and I should be happy. The town was celebrating and here I was being all moody.

"It is good," I replied firmly. "Like I said to Missy at lunch, everything can get back to normal now. That means getting back to my spreadsheets and purchase orders. I'd better get back to work."

Terrence began to slowly fade. *"Bye, Tedi. See you later."*

And with another whoosh of cool air, he was gone. I'm not sure I'm ever going to get used to that.

I put on another pair of shoes – this pair far more comfortable – and headed directly for my office and my neglected work. I'd had ten thousand excuses this last week for avoiding it but that was all over. I had an inn to run and I'd best get to it.

I didn't make it all the way, however. I ran into Cherie coming out of the dining room. She waved me down before I could duck into my office.

"Tedi, I wanted to say thank you for moving me into another room. It really has been so helpful. I do think that I will be checking out tomorrow morning and heading home to my friends and family. Roger's parents need me."

I'd moved Cherie into a quiet corner of the inn so she could get some rest, but also because Jack's deputies had taped off the Bergstroms' and Adam Taylor's rooms. They also wanted access to Roger's possessions.

"I'm glad I could help," I replied, noticing that her eyes were still red and puffy. I felt so badly for her. She'd come for a fun weekend and now her entire world had exploded. "Is there anything I can get for you? Let me know and I'll have it sent up to your room."

Cherie shook her head. "No, nothing – Wait, there is something you can do for me. I need to get into my old room but there's yellow tape across the door."

"The police did that but I'm sure it's only temporary. Did you leave something in the room? I can call the sheriff and he can have one of his deputies get it for you."

"No, that's fine. I can get it when they release the room. I just wanted something of Roger's...I thought it might help. Maybe it's for the best. It might make things worse."

"I can call–"

"Really, it's okay. It was a silly idea, anyway. A shirt that smells like him isn't going to replace the Roger I knew."

That was really sweet. Cherie was a heck of a lot more forgiving than I would have been under the circumstances. Roger had been having an affair with her best friend, after all.

"Just let me know if you change your mind. Jack or one of his deputies can be out here in minutes."

Or they could give me permission to go into the room. I wouldn't touch anything.

"I'll keep that in mind. Thank you. I think I'll go upstairs and try to rest."

"That's a good idea. I can send dinner up to you as well."

"I think that would be good. I can feel everyone looking at me."

"I'm sure they're not."

Boy, that was a huge lie but I was trying to make her feel better.

She gave me a watery smile. "Perhaps it's only my imagination. Still, I think I would be more comfortable eating in my room tonight."

"No problem. Just let the kitchen know what you'd like and we'll send it up."

Cherie thanked me and left, so I had no choice but to sit down and work. I had to give Jack credit. Two murders in one week and he'd wrapped them up as quickly as he'd said he would. He'd also done it without alienating the entire town. He might work out after all.

Chapter Twenty-Three

DESPITE ALL OF the distractions, I'd been incredibly productive. For the last several hours I'd checked item after item off of my to-do list. It was satisfying but it also built up a healthy appetite. I was starving. Missy had her book club tonight so I decided to grab a bite in the kitchen. Delicious aromas from the dinner service had been wafting through the door while I worked and my stomach was in full-on growling mode. If I didn't feed it soon, it might make enough noise for the guests on the top floor to hear me.

I was surprised to see Jack and his son Tyler sitting in my dining room perusing menus. For some reason I thought Jack would be stuck at the station but he'd caught the killers, so that probably meant he could relax a little. There was no better way to do that than with a plate of my chef's deep-dish apple pie. It was the dessert special tonight and I was planning on having a big slice. A la mode.

Tyler gave me a big smile and a wave when he saw me and I waved back, deciding that it would be rude not to stop and chat at least for a moment. The fact was I really wanted to hear about the case and not from the gossip mill, but I also didn't want to appear overeager like a murder-groupie.

"How are you this evening?" I asked in my best professional voice. "Has someone taken your drink orders yet?"

Jack placed his menu on the table. "Andrea took our drink orders, thank you. What do you recommend this evening?"

"The trout is good and I would definitely save room for the apple pie."

But if you don't, then there's more for me.

Tyler was already turning up his nose at the trout suggestion. "I think I'm going to have a cheeseburger."

"Another excellent choice. I think that's what I'm going to have tonight, too."

Andrea dropped off two sodas, her pen in her hand ready to take their order. "Are you dining with them, Tedi? Can I bring you an iced tea?"

This whole town was determined that I wouldn't stay single and now they were pushing us to dine together. At least it wasn't romantic in the slightest. Tyler was here and the dining room was well-lit and lively.

"Please join us, Tedi," Jack said, nodding toward the empty seats. They'd been seated at a four-top so there was room.

He was only being polite.

"I don't want to intrude."

"Nonsense," Jack replied briskly. "It will be nice to actually talk to a human being. Tyler just stares at his phone the entire time."

"I'm playing a game," the teen protested. "I'm not staring."

"Playing, staring, it all looks the same, son." He looked back up at me. "Seriously, you shouldn't eat by yourself in the kitchen."

It would be churlish to refuse and besides, I really wanted to hear about the case from the source itself.

"If you're sure…"

"We're sure."

I sat next to Tyler who had given up his menu and was now, indeed, looking at his phone. Andrea took our orders and quickly brought me a tea from the beverage station. The chilled liquid felt good on my parched throat. I'd not only worked up an appetite, I'd worked up a thirst, too. I'd been too busy to get a refill this afternoon.

Jack wanted conversation so I decided to start one. A nice neutral subject.

"I would have thought you'd be home handing out Halloween candy," I remarked, taking another sip of my tea. "Did anyone tell you it's Halloween?"

There were several people in the dining room in costume and all of my staff had dressed up as well. Andrea was wearing a lab coat and a stethoscope.

"I did notice it but I made sure my porch light was turned off and we came here for dinner."

"That's a good way to get your windows soaped and your trees TP'd."

Jack only smirked at my remark. "I'm the sheriff, Tedi. No

one is going to do that."

He really didn't have a clue.

"Would you like to make it interesting? I've got five bucks that says you're going to wake up to Charmin waving in the wind. It's supposed to rain tonight, too."

His eyes narrowed and his lips turned up slightly at the corners. An almost smile.

"I don't think five bucks is all that interesting. How about twenty?"

If Jack thought I was going to back down, he was mistaken.

I held out my hand. "You're on."

He shook it but that superior expression was still there. "How come you aren't giving out candy? Aren't you worried about having your windows soaped?"

"We don't do that here at the inn. We already threw a killer of a party."

Is it too soon? Okay, it's too soon. I've always had a sort of morbid sense of humor and would make jokes in uncomfortable situations.

"Very funny. You should be a comedian."

"I really should. I'm incredibly talented."

A total lie. I had no discernible talent at all. I couldn't even whistle. When I was a kid, I'd always been in charge of lights or scenery whenever we put on a play. When I was five and the class learned to play "Hot Cross Buns" on the recorder, I flunked.

I think you get the idea. But I have plenty more examples.

Just let me know.

"So…how was your day?" I asked oh so casually. "I kind of expected you to still be at the station."

Jack glanced at Tyler who was heads down over his phone. "If you want the details, Tedi, you only have to ask."

Well…fine.

"Okay, I'm asking."

Jack shrugged as if putting two people behind bars for murder was an everyday occurrence.

"You probably know most of it already. The state police pulled Lorna Bergstrom and Adam Taylor over because I'd put out a BOLO. We needed to speak to Lorna after finding Roger this morning."

"Gossip is saying that they were going to visit a friend."

"That was their story," Jack agreed. "But I'm not buying it."

"Oh?"

Rubbing his chin, he glanced at his son, absorbed in his video game. He leaned forward so only I could hear, lowering his voice. "There's a piece of evidence that we haven't made public."

"To anyone?"

"No one. The state police told me about it but I haven't shared the details with my deputies, the press, or anyone else, for that matter."

Now I totally wanted to know the details.

"But you're going to tell me, right?"

Chuckling, he shook his head. "No, I am not."

"I won't tell anyone."

"Actually, I believe you. As I've said before, you're about the only halfway normal person in this town. But I'm still not going to tell you."

Tyler put his phone down on the table and stood. "I'm going to the bathroom."

"You say 'Excuse me, I'm going to the bathroom', son."

"Excuse me, I'm going to the bathroom, son."

I coughed behind my hand to hide my laughter. Tyler was a funny kid.

"You're excused."

Tyler turned and wandered off in the general direction of the facilities. I had a feeling he wasn't going to hurry back from the way he looked at the pretty girl at table seven. She also attended Ravenmist High School.

"I'm a terrible father."

"You're fine," I assured him. "He's a happy, normal teenager."

"Who hates my guts for moving him out of Chicago."

"All teenagers have moments where they hate their parents guts. It's a rite of passage."

Jack's phone buzzed and he quickly checked it, smiling at whatever it was.

"Good news?"

"You could say that."

"Spill it. Just spill it, for heaven's sake. I won't tell anybody and I can tell that you're dying to tell me. Admit it."

He looked at his phone again and then sighed. "By tomorrow morning it won't be a secret anymore. I'm holding a press conference in the town square so I can answer questions."

"So you'll tell me? I won't rat you out."

Maybe I've watched too many James Cagney movies.

"Okay but keep it to yourself. The two suspects were belligerent and difficult when they were pulled over but did give the police the permission to search the vehicle. That's when a bloody knife was found and it was immediately taken to the state lab and a rush has been put on it. It will be checked to see if it matches the wounds on either victim and it will also be processed for DNA and fingerprints. In the meantime, we can hold them without charges for at least twenty-four hours, maybe longer because this is a serious crime. That's why the lab has put a rush on the testing."

Lorna was driving around Central Illinois with a murder weapon in the trunk?

"It doesn't make any sense."

"Which part? Lorna had motive to kill her husband."

"But not Roger," I argued. "Why would she kill him?"

Another shrug. "Maybe she wanted him to leave his wife and he wouldn't. Maybe they argued. I'm not all that concerned with her motive, to be honest. That's for a prosecutor to worry about. I will say this, though. Whomever committed these murders didn't do them in a moment of passion. They put some thought in it."

"How so?"

"Generally, people don't die from stab wounds. A person has

to be stabbed in a few specific areas of their body for that to happen. The killer did their homework. They knew exactly what they were doing. Bergstrom was stabbed in the neck and then drowned in water. Mullaney was stabbed under the arm where there's a major artery."

"Lorna wouldn't have known any of that."

"Ever heard of the internet? You can look up anything on there."

"Fine, then how about the knife in the trunk? Why on earth would she put the knife in the trunk? And then allow the police to search the car? That doesn't make sense either."

It really didn't.

"Maybe she didn't know it was there. Taylor might have placed it in the trunk. Or maybe she didn't think the police would find it. I don't know, but I do know that we have reason to suspect them of a double murder." He gave her a shrewd look. "You doubt their guilt?"

"I dunno," I sighed. "It just seems…flimsy."

To my shock and utter surprise, Jack nodded in agreement. "I agree. That's why I'm not charging them with anything yet. I'm waiting for the forensics and the state lab owes me a few favors from when I was back in Chicago. We need to know for sure. Right now, Bergstrom and Taylor are swearing they're innocent."

"They might be."

"They might be, but might I remind you that most people in prison say that they're innocent. They were also caught with a bloody knife in the trunk of their car and the second victim wrote Lorna's name on the wall. That's a huge clue."

News of the bloody writing had made it around Ravenmist in record time and had pretty much sealed the town's opinion of Lorna.

"If Roger did it. The killer could have done it to throw off the police." I pointed to Jack. "That would be you."

"I agree that could be a possibility. That's why the lab is checking out the writing. If Roger wrote it, they'll be able to tell us. But that sort of analysis takes weeks. They can do fingerprints fast but DNA takes much more time."

Slightly deflated, I sat back in my chair. "I thought you'd argue with me."

Chuckling, Jack rubbed at the stubble on his chin. "Sorry about that. I do agree that we need more evidence, but in the meantime, I would be foolish to let those two out so they could flee the state. As far as I'm concerned, they're a flight risk, although they claim they were only going to visit a friend."

"They did leave all of their belongings at the inn."

"There are explanations for that too, Tedi."

"I know. I think this whole murder thing has thrown me. We don't normally have violence in Ravenmist. It's not something we ever worry about, frankly."

"I hope that once this is over the town can go back to that," Jack replied earnestly. "But the world is a dangerous place, Tedi. You can't shut your eyes to it."

Danger must have been the magic word to get Tyler back to

the table because he groaned and rolled his eyes as he sat down. "Dad thinks there's danger around every corner. He's sure that everyone is a violent psychopath."

"I'm just cautious. You should be, too."

Far be it for me to get between a father and a son, so I stayed quiet.

"When are we going ghost hunting again, Tedi?" Tyler asked. Apparently, ghosts were cooler than video games. "I heard that the inn was haunted. Can we investigate here?"

"Maybe," I said, thinking about Terrence but also about Edward. He'd said that there were lots of ghosts all over Ravenmist and that they were beginning to have more energy. They were "waking up" in a way, able to show themselves when they couldn't before. "There are lots of places in town that are said to have spirits. I'll call a meeting next week and we can talk about it. Choose our next location."

Andrea slid our plates in front of us, the smell of hot food making my stomach growl again. I really was hungry. It was going to be a struggle not to wolf down my food. My mother would be appalled.

"You're welcome to investigate the sheriff's office," Jack offered with a grin. "Your group can clean out some old, dusty files while you're at it."

"Does that mean that you're resigning from the club?"

"Not in the least. The Ravenmist Paranormal Investigation Society is stuck with me."

This could become a sticky situation. Since ghosts were real, eventually Mr. Non-Believer was going to see a real honest to goodness ghost.

What would the smirking jerk do then?

Chapter Twenty-Four

I WAS STILL thinking about my conversation with Jack later that night as the dining room closed down and the bar livened up. The patrons were going to be there until last call, I was sure of it. Already it was loud with laughter and music. Many of the customers were in costume and the whole evening had a festive air. There was much to celebrate as Lorna and Adam were behind bars.

Jerome and Roger. Two victims. What did they have in common?

The obvious answer was Lorna. She was the link between the two men and that was what bugged me. I'd watched more than my share of television crime shows and the spouse was always the first to be suspected. If Lorna was going to murder her husband, she should have had a better alibi than she'd been *sleeping*.

And then the whole knife in the trunk. Just how dumb was Lorna? If she was smart enough to kill two men, one would imagine that she'd be smart enough to at least *try* and hide her crime.

Jack had said that the killer had been intelligent enough to do their homework, learning exactly where to stab someone to kill them. I certainly had no idea where the best place to do that was located on the human body. They made it look so easy in the movies. A knife in the back…and then dead. Apparently, it wasn't that simple.

After checking with the kitchen staff that we were ready for breakfast tomorrow morning, I headed to my little apartment. It had been one incredibly long day and all I wanted to do was soak in a hot tub and sip a glass of wine while I watched an old movie.

Not *Strangers on a Train*. Nope. No murder. Something happier instead. Perhaps a little Fred and Ginger might help my mood. *Top Hat*, anyone?

I said goodnight to Andrea who was clearing off the table-cloths and tossing them into a giant hamper on wheels when I looked out of the window to the back patio and saw the glowing tip of a cigarette. Someone was smoking and I didn't allow it that close to the building. The designated smoking area was the gazebo on the side of the inn and for the most part guests were good about following the rules. I'd just ask this one nicely to move.

The glare on the windows from the lights hadn't allowed me to see which guest it was but now that I was outside, the cold seeping into my bones and making me rub at my sweater-clad arms, I could see that it was Cherie. She was leaning against the black wrought iron railing, her elbows resting on the metal and her gaze staring out somewhere far away. I didn't have to wonder what she was thinking about.

"Mrs. Mullaney."

Cherie took a long drag on the cigarette and then exhaled, the blue smoke curling around her head. I had to steel myself not to wrinkle my nose in distaste. Smoking was one of my pet peeves and my parents had to talk me out of banning it altogether from the inn.

My ex used to smoke cigars every now and then just to annoy me.

"Hello, Tedi. I thought I told you to call me Cherie."

"Cherie," I repeated dutifully. I cleared my throat, hating having to bring the old hammer down but I didn't want cigarette smoke this close to the exits. "I'm afraid I'm going to have to ask you to move to the gazebo. That's the only place we allow smoking here. I am sorry."

I wasn't all that sorry actually, but I was sorry that I had to tell her when she'd been through so much.

She held up her cigarette. "I quit for awhile but now I'm back to smoking. Do you smoke?"

I shook my head. "No, I don't."

Mom and Dad would have had a cow if I'd smoked. My parents were sticklers for clear lungs.

"Good. It's a nasty habit. Roger always hated it."

I didn't know what to say, especially since she'd brought up her now deceased husband. I didn't need to worry about it, though. She was happy to do that talking.

"He made me quit when we started dating. I've started back

up now and then through the years but I always stopped again."

"That's good. Quitting, I mean."

"I should never have started," Cherie said with a sigh, blowing out a billow of smoke. "It was the stress from my job that got me into it. I worked as an emergency room nurse before I married Roger. Very hectic and often tragic. The stress got to me and next thing I knew I had started smoking. Roger, of course, hated it and I wanted to please him so I quit."

"You were a nurse?"

Cherie smiled sadly and tossed her cigarette down on the concrete, pressing on it with her shoe. "For twelve years in one of the busiest emergency rooms in Chicago. Then I married Roger and he didn't want me to work. I held onto my job for a while but eventually I quit."

A nurse. Cherie was a nurse. She had extensive medical training.

She'd know where to place a knife because she would have seen multiple stab wounds in her job.

It wasn't the cold air that sent a chill down my spine but this woman standing next to me. I needed to call Jack. He needed to talk to Cherie before she left town in the morning.

I rubbed the goosebumps on my arms, my teeth chattering. I'm an idiot who didn't have the sense to put on a coat. "What will you do now?"

Cherie was looking out onto the large backyard again. "Go home. Try and pick up the pieces of my life."

"You must be angry with Lorna."

"I wouldn't waste the emotion on her. She'll get what she deserves."

"What's that?"

"The rest of her life in prison to think about what she's done."

"She might not be guilty. The evidence isn't conclusive."

An eyebrow raised, Cherie snorted. "I would think a bloody knife wrapped up in my husband's jacket would be pretty conclusive."

If Cherie's earlier statement about being a nurse had sent a chill up my spine, this one stopped my blood cold. According to Jack, the one detail no one knew was that the police had found a knife in the trunk of the car. She shouldn't know this unless...

Cherie had killed her husband.

Cold sweat had pooled on the back of my neck and under my arms. I was standing next to a killer.

What do I do now?

Chapter Twenty-Five

THAT LITTLE VOICE in my head whispered to stay calm and cool. Don't show how rattled I actually am. The test of my acting skills started now.

"I didn't realize Jack had told you about the knife. They're keeping that quiet."

Without a moment's hesitation, Cherie looked me right in the eye and lied. "Yes, he told me when I met with him this afternoon. I am the widow, after all."

"It's good that you have all of the details." I needed to call Jack. Right away. "It's getting cold out here. I think I'll go inside. Are you headed to bed? It's getting late."

I didn't wait for Cherie to answer, hurrying inside the much warmer building. It felt almost stifling in my overheated state, and I tugged at the collar of my sweater, trying to cool myself off. Sending a glance over my shoulder to ensure that I hadn't been followed, I walked calmly to my office and grabbed my phone off of my desk, my shaking fingers stumbling to dial.

"I can't let you do that."

Well...shoot. I wasn't as cool and sly as I thought I was.

Huge surprise. Cherie must have run after me to get here so fast. I froze, my heart slamming against my ribs and roaring in my ears.

Don't show any emotion. Don't show fear.

Wait…was that for killers or bears? I couldn't remember.

Turning to face Cherie, I plastered a big fake smile on my face. "Hey, Cherie. Was there something else you needed? I think there's some apple pie left from dinner."

"You know."

This is where my complete inexperience with murder handicapped me. Did I play dumb or did I brazen it out? Cherie didn't appear to have a weapon but I couldn't be sure. Her hands were in her coat pockets. She could have another knife or worse, a gun. I wasn't ready to die. I had too many things I needed to do first.

"Know what? I'm not sure what you're talking about. Is everything okay?"

I guess I'd decided to play dumb. My fight or flight instinct was kicking right in and I wanted to run but Cherie was standing between me and the doorway.

"You know I killed Roger."

I couldn't play dumb now. Why did killers confess anyway? Did they feel guilty or did they want to brag?

"I don't know anything, Cherie. You should lie down. I think you're overtired."

Cherie's lips flattened into a line and her eyes flashed with anger. "My best friend in the whole world was sleeping with my husband. She was my *best friend*. She'd taken everything from me that I ever cared about. So I decided to take everything from her. I killed her husband and Roger, and I made sure that she'd be blamed for it. She'll sit in a cell for the rest of her life thinking about what she did to me while I live in freedom and luxury."

I couldn't stop the words tumbling from my mouth. "You killed your own husband to get back at Lorna?"

"That cheating bastard deserved to die."

"What about you forgiving him and buying a house here in Ravenmist?"

"That was never going to happen. It was simply to divert suspicion from me."

Sweat rolled down my back, making my wool sweater stick to my skin. I wanted to scratch at the flesh but I didn't dare move my hands, wanting Cherie to stay as calm as possible. The less I moved, the less she might move.

What could she do? The inn was full of people. They were mostly asleep but a few of the kitchen staff were still around and the front desk clerk was on duty. We weren't alone and clearly she didn't have a plan. Jack had said that the other murders were thought out. This? This wasn't. It gave me a slight advantage.

Hopefully.

"Why did you do it in Ravenmist? Why come all of the way here?"

I was hoping if I kept Cherie talking I might somehow talk her out of whatever she was planning to do to me. I knew her secret so she couldn't let me live.

"A backwater town with a backwater cop in charge. I did my homework. This stupid little town hasn't had a murder in ages. Your sheriff will take the evidence I've given him and do the right thing. Arrest Lorna."

"What about Adam?"

"What about him?"

"He's innocent."

"No one in this world is innocent, least of all Adam. He's been helping Jerry cover up his theft for years."

"So Jerome really was stealing from his partner."

"Jerry was a philandering thief and the world is a better place without him. No one is going to mourn his passing."

"You've thought it all through."

"I've been planning this for two years, and I'm not going to let you ruin this for me." She reached out and tried to grab my arm but I jerked away just in time. "Don't fight me. This is inevitable."

I begged to differ. Did this broad actually think I was going to go without a tussle? She had to be out of her mind to think I was just going to give up and go quietly. Unless she had a hidden weapon, I had a decent shot at winning a wrestling match with her.

"There are people in this inn who will hear me if I scream," I warned, taking two steps back. There wasn't much room to maneuver in this small space and my back was against the metal filing cabinets. I was trapped but still defiant. This was not how I was going to go out. Missy wasn't getting a text tonight. At least not about me. "And I will scream this place down like Jamie Lee Curtis in a horror flick."

This time Cherie didn't go for my arm. Her hand wrapped around the plant on my desk, Howard the Fern. It had a heavy earthenware pot that could easily crack my skull open like an egg. Dodging to the left and hoping she'd go right, I felt that familiar cold wave run over me and then Terrence was in the room, zipping around like a ghost on speed. Cherie screamed and dropped the plant to the floor where it loudly shattered into a thousand pieces, leaving a mess on the maple planks. With another scream she turned and ran out of my office as if the hounds of hell were at her heels. Terrence had scared the bejesus out of her.

And probably saved my life, although I like to think that I could have taken a middle-aged housewife in hand to hand combat. Did I mention that I'd gone to the gym about six months ago? I'd had a great workout and been sore for days.

Terrence came to rest on my desk, his expression a mask of worried concern. *"Are you okay?"*

Breathless, I nodded, not able to trust my voice yet. I sucked in a few lungfuls of oxygen before I could speak.

"Thank you. How did you know I was in trouble?"

"I told you before, I watch. I watched over Rose and now I watch over you."

It was literally the sweetest thing a ghost had ever said to me. I wanted to hug him but I wasn't sure if I should, could, or even if he'd want me to.

So I did it anyway. I wrapped my arms around Terrence, feeling the zips of electricity tingle through my fingers all the way to my ears.

"You're a good friend."

Another cold wave and Terrence was gone out of my sight, replaced by the looming figure of Sheriff Jackson Garrett. He looked none too happy, by the way. Had he witnessed my hug with Terrence and then subsequent disappearance?

Jack's voice was low but calm. "Can someone tell me what's going on here?"

"Cherie is the real killer. She just tried to kill me, too."

He glanced down at the demolished potted fern. Poor Howard.

"She ran out of here," I said urgently, coming around the desk to push at his shoulder. He was so solid he didn't budge. He might as well have been a tree. "You have to go after her. She's getting away."

"We already have her. My deputies are taking her into custody right now."

But how...? "I don't understand. How did you know that she was trying to kill me?"

Jack sighed and shook his head. "I didn't. That was pure luck. I got a text from the state lab that they found one partial fingerprint on the knife. Cherie Mullaney. Her prints were in the system because she'd done some volunteer work at a high school. I also got word from my contact in Chicago that she took out a million-dollar insurance policy on her husband about six months ago. That was enough to get my attention. I was coming to pick her up when she ran screaming and yelling right out of your front door and bang, right into me."

About that…

"That's good then."

I sat down on the edge of the desk, the adrenaline draining from my body, leaving me limp and exhausted. It had been one heck of day. Where was that glass of wine and hot bath I'd been dreaming about?

"Are you going to be okay? I need to get back to work."

Blinking a few times, I had to run Jack's words through my head again to comprehend them. My brain was officially mush.

"Sure. Yeah. I'm good. Go ahead."

He didn't appear convinced. "Are you sure? You look pale."

"Because a woman tried to kill me with a fern a few minutes ago. That doesn't happen to me every day." I took a fortifying breath and waved him away. "Seriously, I'm good. Fine. Go ahead."

"I'll need your statement but it can wait until morning."

"Okay."

He took a step toward the door and then hesitated. "I can have a deputy come sit with you."

"I'm all good."

Reaching into his pocket, he pulled out his phone. "I'm calling Missy for you. You shouldn't be by yourself."

That was an excellent idea. Missy. She'd known what to say or do.

"Thank you."

He spoke softly into the phone and then hung up. "She's on her way."

"It won't take her five minutes to get here, Jack. You can go. You've got a killer to deal with."

The real one this time.

"She's not going anywhere."

I looked up at him and our gazes met. I saw a heck of a lot of worry in those blue eyes. Unneeded worry, in my estimation. I'd be fine just as soon as my heart and breathing went back to normal.

"Neither am I. Go take a victory lap, Sheriff. You earned this one."

We both did.

For a long moment, I didn't think Jack was going to go but he eventually turned and left leaving me sitting on my desk with Howard the Fern massacred on the floor.

I didn't know how long I sat there, slightly numb but Missy walked in, took one look at the office, and bundled me out of there. All the while I protested about Howard the Fern but Missy said she'd get me a new Howard.

My mom was going to be so upset about Howard. That's when I realized it...

"You can't tell my mom what happened. She'll freak out."

"Your mom is going to find out what really happened," Missy said patiently, pushing open the door to my apartment. "The whole town is going to know. You helped catch a killer.

You're a hero."

A hero? No way. Terrence was the hero but no one would ever know that.

"I don't want to be a hero."

"Too late. The whole town is going to be talking about how you exposed a murderer. I bet you'll get a free meal at Daisy's."

If it was chicken and dumplings, that would be awesome.

Chapter Twenty-Six

L ORNA AND ADAM put their last suitcase in the trunk of the car before pulling me into such a tight hug I could barely breathe. They'd been released from jail this morning after Cherie had confessed, plus the forensics that had come back from the state lab. The DNA would take much longer but the partial print that Cherie had failed to clean off the knife told the tale.

"I don't know how to thank you and the sheriff," Lorna said tearfully, her voice thick with emotion. "I could have spent the rest of my life in prison."

"I didn't do anything," I assured her, my face growing warm. "I was just in the right place at the right time."

Or the wrong place at the wrong time, depending on how you looked at it.

"Your statement to the sheriff helped," Lorna replied firmly. "And I am grateful. We both are."

Adam's face was about as red as mine was but he nodded awkwardly, the car keys jangling between his fingers. He wanted to leave and I couldn't blame him. This town hadn't been a vacation paradise for either one of these people.

"What happens now?" I asked Lorna as Adam opened the passenger door. "What will you do?"

Sighing, Lorna's eyes filled with more tears. "I'm not sure. Jerry was stealing from his partner so I assume we don't have any money. He must have spent it all. I guess I'll have to get a job. It won't be so bad. At least I won't be in prison."

"That's true. There are worse things than working for a living."

A car pulled up next to theirs and I tensed when I saw who was driving it. Angela. This could go sideways really fast. What was she thinking coming here?

Angela jumped out of the vehicle and ran around the hood to stand in front of Lorna.

"I'm so glad I caught you before you left." Angela paused before continuing. "I wanted to say that I'm sorry. Really sorry."

Angela didn't say anything else and I held my breath waiting for Lorna's response. They had shouted at each other not long ago so I didn't have much hope that this encounter would be any better, but Lorna simply nodded in return.

"Thank you."

No shouting. No name calling.

Angela fumbled in her pocket and pulled out a piece of paper. "I wanted to give this to you. Jerry was hiding money from you. He told me about it. He has an account in the Cayman Islands. I thought you might need it."

Lorna accepted the slip of paper with a smile. "I do, thank you."

Without another word Angela turned and climbed back into her car, driving away.

I pointed to the paper. "Maybe things won't be so dire after all."

"Maybe," Lorna said. "But I think I still want to get a job. I want to be useful. Besides, this money probably belongs to Wagner."

Adam placed his hand on Lorna's shoulder. "Are you ready to go?"

"I am."

The two of them drove away, waving and smiling as they disappeared down the road. It felt good that two innocent people were going free to live their lives.

Back in my office I was surprised to see Jack leaning against my desk, examining the repotted Howard the Fern. Missy had stopped by this morning and with hope, luck, and water he would survive.

I hadn't expected to see Jack again this morning. I would have thought he'd be busy at the station after I'd given him my statement.

"Where is your SUV?"

"I parked it out back. I didn't think Lorna and Adam wanted to see me again."

"That's true," I conceded. "They say they'll come back for the Fall Festival next year but I'll be shocked if they do. How's Cherie?"

"I took her full statement this morning and now it's up to

the forensics lab and the prosecutors. Cherie's going to be transferred this afternoon to the county lock up. She pretty much admitted everything. Her whole plan was to come here to a small town where the police resources wouldn't be experienced in murder and frame Lorna. She planted the knife in the trunk as you know. She wrote Lorna's name on the wall and she also impersonated her when she stabbed Bergstrom. She wore a wig in case anyone saw her, which no one did."

"That explains—"

I broke off, not wanting to say out loud that Terrence had seen "Lorna" that morning. But from a distance he couldn't tell that it was Cherie.

"Explains what?"

"Nothing. Nothing at all. So it's all over. What a relief. Unless there's something else you want to discuss with me?"

Tense, I waited for his verdict. Just what had he seen last night?

His eyes narrowed and he rubbed his chin. "Not that I can think of. Why? Did you have something you wanted to talk about, Tedi?"

"Nope. Nothing."

"Then it's all good."

I'm not sure I would call it good. Weird? Yes. Good? Maybe.

"How about I fix you a late lunch, Sheriff? On the house."

"I wouldn't turn that down." He reached into his pocket and pulled out a twenty-dollar bill. "And I think I owe you this."

I respected a man who paid his debts.

"They toilet-papered your trees."

I didn't make it sound like a question.

"They'll regret it."

"You'll never find out who did it."

"I just solved a double murder, Tedi. I think I can find a couple of kids with a six-pack of toilet paper."

"If you say so. Now how about that lunch?"

I wasn't going to bring up that moment in the office again. It was best to simply leave it alone. Sheriff Jack Garrett was in denial. He either didn't see anything or he didn't want to talk about it. Interesting.

I'd been given a reprieve. For now.

I hope you enjoyed Eat, Drink, and Be Scary! Don't miss the next mystery in the Ravenmist Whodunit series – Ghoul You Be My Valentine?

Thank you for reading.

Don't miss a thing! Sign up to be notified of Olivia's new releases:

Mailing List

http://eepurl.com/gdVe3T

About The Author

Olivia Jaymes is a wife, mother, lover of sexy romance and cozy mysteries, and caffeine addict. She lives with her husband, son, and two spoiled dogs in central Florida and spends her days typing on her computer with a canine on her lap.

She is currently working on a new cozy mystery series – *A Ravenmist Whodunit* – in addition to her other ongoing romance series.

Visit Olivia Jaymes at

www.OliviaJaymes.com